The radio child actress ran up to Flossie.
"You are my double!" she cried delightedly.

The Bobbsey Twins in a Radio Play

The Bobbsey Twins in a Radio Play

By
LAURA LEE HOPE

Author of
THE BOBBSEY TWINS SERIES

GROSSET & DUNLAP
Publishers   New York

The Bobbsey Twins in a Radio Play

CONTENTS

THE BOBBSEY TWINS IN A RADIO PLAY

CHAPTER I

A MYSTERIOUS VISITOR

"Jump! Jump, Waggo!"

Bert Bobbsey snapped his fingers, and the little fox terrier leaped over a row of chairs which the boy had placed upside down in the living room. The dog was young and very eager to please, so he did the trick several times.

"That's good, Waggo," approved Bert. "How would you like to learn to slide down our banister next?"

The little animal barked joyfully at this idea. He wagged his stump of a tail and frisked about excitedly.

"I guess I'd better pick up these chairs first, before you do any more stunts," murmured the Bobbsey boy, setting to work.

1

"Bow wow, Bow wow," answered the pet dog, darting back and forth over the furniture as his young master tried to put things in order.

"Down, Waggo!" Bert commanded. "You'll wake up Snap first thing you know."

Now Snap, as some of my readers will remember, was the Bobbseys' old dog. He had always lived an active and exciting life. Now he liked nothing so well as peace and quiet and a comfortable corner where he could drowse away the time without being bothered by anybody. Snap seemed older than usual on this particular day. He lay on the rug before the hearth, his head between his paws, and watched young Waggo out of half-closed eyes.

The young dog, full of mischief, could not understand why Snap liked to be alone. Whenever he wanted to be friendly and draw the other animal into his romps, the old dog would just look bored and then walk away.

Now, as Bert mentioned his name, Snap raised his head and yawned. Waggo made a pass at him, but the old dog merely closed his jaws with a click.

There came a merry laugh from the doorway, and Nan, Bert's pretty twin sister, came into the room. "Poor old Snap," she said, laying a hand on the Bobbsey pet. "He can't even yawn in peace. Waggo must be a terrible trial to him."

"Do him good to be waked up once in a while," said Bert unfeelingly. "The only thing he does is lie around the house all day and snore. Now Waggo, he's some fun. We were just going through his tricks when you came in. Want to watch him act, Nan?"

His twin sister sat down on the hearth rug beside Snap. She pushed her pretty brown hair back from her face and prepared to enjoy the show.

"Go ahead," she invited. "Anyway, even if Waggo *is* smart, I still like old Snap better," she added loyally, patting the old dog.

Whether Waggo was offended by this remark, or, which is more probable, he was merely tired out with his previous efforts, the fact remains that he positively refused to do any more tricks that day. Nan coaxed, Bert commanded and even threatened; still Waggo would not sit up and beg, roll over and play dead, or do any other of the numerous stunts which Bert so patiently had taught him.

"I've never seen him so stupid before," said Bert; then added with a half-sheepish grin, "I guess if there is going to be a show I'll have to put it on myself."

"Go ahead," said Nan with a laugh. "I'd love to see you sit up and beg or roll over and play dead. I'm sure Snap and Waggo would enjoy it too," she added.

Bert grinned good-naturedly.

"I can do something better than that to entertain them," he offered. "Do you know I can bark like a dog?"

"No, can you?" asked Nan, only half believing him. "Go ahead. It should be interesting, even for the dogs."

Bert began by imitating young Waggo's excited yapping, and ended with Snap's hoarse baying.

The performance was too much for the dogs. At Bert's first sound Waggo joined him, rushing about the room in wild excitement, barely avoiding a collision with chair and table legs. Old Snap tried hard to close his ears to all the noise, but when Bert began to imitate his own wheezing bark the old dog forgot to be tired and joined in the loud uproar.

Nan hugged herself and laughed until the tears rolled down her face. "What a show," she cried.

Into this wild hubbub rushed colored Dinah, the Bobbseys' faithful old servant. She had a broom in one hand with which she made a lunge at Waggo as he passed by her. The young dog evidently thought that the woman wanted to play with him, for he seized the broom between his teeth and gave it a joyful tug.

"Hi, you dawg!" cried the colored cook so she could be heard above the racket. "What you-all doin' wiv my broom? Stop that, you hear me?"

Poor Dinah! Even as she spoke her foot caught in the edge of a rumpled rug and she fell flat, while the broom hurtled from her hand and struck a bookcase at the far side of the room.

"Ho! Ho!" cried little Freddie Bobbsey who came through the doorway with his twin sister Flossie. "What did you do that for, Dinah?"

With Nan's help the colored woman had struggled to a sitting position. Now she looked coldly at Freddie and Flossie, who were viewing the scene and laughing merrily.

"Ah s'pose you-all thinks Ah enjoys this," she grumbled, casting a suspicious glance at Nan, who was trying her very best to keep from laughing. "Ah s'pose you-all think it's mighty funny."

"It was just like a play," said Flossie happily, clapping her hands. "Bert, you bark some more. And Dinah, please fall again."

The cook's horrified look at this suggestion was too much for Nan and Bert, who went off into gales of laughter. After a moment Dinah's mouth began to twitch and then she too joined her rich chuckle to theirs.

"Well, anyway, it *was* like a play," Flossie insisted. "And I wish Dinah would do it again."

Suddenly into the confusion there came the sharp peal of the front doorbell. With Nan's help Dinah struggled hurriedly to her feet. She gave a hopeless look about the untidy room before starting for the door.

"Chilluns and dawgs belongs outside," she grumbled. "Allus stirrin' up trouble inside de house, seems like."

Flossie followed Dinah to the door, and so was the first one to see the pretty lady standing on the porch.

"Do the Haymans live here?" asked a kind voice. "I believe I have the right address."

"No, ma'am, no Haymans lives here," said Dinah. "Looks lak you mus' have de wrong street."

As the stranger seemed greatly puzzled Nan took matters into her own hands. "Our name is Bobbsey," she said. "We don't know anyone by the name of Hayman in this neighborhood."

"But here is the address," the woman insisted, holding a slip of paper toward Nan. "I am sure both street and number are correct."

The girl took the paper and looked carefully at what was written on it.

"The address you want is in Lake*view*," she said. "This is Lake*port*."

"What a stupid mistake for me to make!" The

woman's brows drew together in a frown. "Perhaps you will let me look in your telephone directory so that I can make sure the Haymans really live at this address," she ventured.

Flossie came forward with the book. The stranger took off her gloves and thumbed through the sheets rapidly. After a moment she seemed to come to what she was seeking.

"It is right," she said with a smile. "The Haymans' address *is* in Lakeview. Thank you very much. So sorry to have troubled you."

The woman departed breezily with a friendly wave of her hand, and all four of the Bobbsey twins watched her as she stepped into a car and drove off down the street.

"Towns shouldn't have names so nearly alike," grumbled Bert, "especially when they're right next to each other."

"Why don't you tell the mayor about it?" giggled Nan.

She was about to shut the door when her foot came in contact with something hard. She stooped and picked up an object which twinkled brilliantly in the light.

"Why, it's a ring!" said Flossie, standing on tiptoe to peer into Nan's cupped hand. "And such a pretty one. Where do you s'pose it came from?"

"I don't know," said Nan slowly. "It's a diamond, and a beautiful one, but it doesn't look like one of Mother's."

"What doesn't look like one of Mother's?" asked a familiar and well-loved voice from the back of the hallway. "Why Nan," added Mrs. Bobbsey as the children ran forward to greet their mother, "what a beautiful ring you have there! Where did you get it, dear?"

"She found it on the floor," said Flossie.

"Is it yours, Mother?" Freddie asked.

Mrs. Bobbsey took the piece of jewelry from Nan and looked at it carefully.

"No, it isn't mine," she said after a moment.

"Then it must belong to the woman who was here just now," said Bert.

Of course his mother demanded to know what woman Bert meant. He told her.

Mrs. Bobbsey was interested, and suggested that they telephone at once to the house in Lakeview in an effort to get in touch with the woman and learn whether the diamond ring which Nan had found might belong to her. However, the call received no reply.

"Can't we drive over there, Mother?" Bert suggested. "It won't take us long in the car and we may catch up with the stranger."

Mrs. Bobbsey said she thought her son's suggestion a very good one.

"The auto is right out in front," she said, adding with a smile, "Who would like to go with me?"

"I would," cried Flossie, clapping her hands.

"And so would I!" shouted Freddie, making a dash for the front door. "Last one out is a bullfrog!"

There was a scramble for the front door, since no one cared to be called a bullfrog. When the twins finally climbed into the car they were breathless with laughter and unable to decide which one of them had been the last to leave the house.

"I think I was," laughed Mrs. Bobbsey. "That makes me the bullfrog."

Poor Freddie was shocked at the suggestion. "I didn't mean *you*, Mother," he protested. Then he wondered why Nan and Bert and even Flossie laughed at him.

The ride to Lakeview took only a short time, but they did have some trouble in locating the right street and number. When they finally drew up in front of the Hayman house they were sure from its deserted appearance that no one was at home. Moreover, the strange woman was nowhere in sight.

"What shall we do with the valuable ring?" asked Nan, worried.

CHAPTER II

SURPRISE

"THE window shades are all pulled down in the house," said Flossie, pressing her tip-tilted nose against the glass of the car door. "I guess the people who live there will be away for a long time, Mother."

"Well, the thing to do is to make sure of that," said Mrs. Bobbsey briskly. "Bert, will you go ring the doorbell?"

The children watched their brother as he pushed the electric button again and again without getting any answer.

"Shall I go to the next house and ask about the Haymans, Mother?" Nan wanted to know.

Mrs. Bobbsey consented, so her daughter got out of the car and ran up the porch of the adjoining house. A young woman came to the door.

"The Haymans are away on a visit," she replied to Nan's question. "They have been gone some weeks now, and no one seems to be sure just when to expect them back."

Nan told this news to the other Bobbseys and her mother looked a little anxious as she started the motor of the car.

"I *do* wish we might have given back the ring," she said. "I dislike holding valuable property, especially when it belongs to some one else."

"Maybe the strange woman will come back to our house for it," Nan suggested. "If it *is* hers," she added thoughtfully.

At home that evening the twins talked about the ring with Daddy Bobbsey, who felt sure that the unknown lady would return very soon to claim her piece of jewelry.

"You will hear from her by tomorrow at the latest, never fear," Mr. Bobbsey stated.

However, the stranger did not come back for her property the following day, nor the next, nor even the one after that.

The Bobbseys telephoned to the Hayman house each day. They even put an advertisement in the lost-and-found column of a local paper, hoping their mysterious visitor would see it, but all without result.

Nan finally put the ring away in the safest place she could think of, which was in the very bottom of the handkerchief box in her bureau. There it would lie safe until the day she would be able to locate the owner and return her property to her.

One pleasant afternoon later in the week Mr. Bobbsey treated his family to a fine surprise. He brought home a beautiful, shining brand new black car!

"Daddy, is it really ours?" asked Nan unbelievingly.

"Say, it's great, Dad," cried Bert. He walked round and round the auto, admiring its sleek lines, touching the fenders with his fingers, and peering under the hood. "With the very latest of everything, too."

"Glad you like it, Son." Mr. Bobbsey beamed upon his family. He glanced at Mrs. Bobbsey and the two exchanged a mysterious smile. "If we were going anywhere," added Daddy Bobbsey, "we could get there pretty fast in this car, don't you think so?"

Flossie flung herself upon her Daddy and clasped him about the knees.

"Are we going some place?" she cried joyfully. "Oh, Daddy, please say where! Please! Please!" begged the little twin.

Mr. and Mrs. Bobbsey smiled at their children, of whom they are not only very fond, but who are rather unique in one respect. There are two sets of twins in the family. Nan and Bert are the older pair. They are dark-haired and brown-eyed, while Freddie and Flossie, their younger twin brother and sister, are blonde and blue-eyed—and very mischievous.

They live in Lakeport, where Daddy Bobbsey is in the lumber business. Their two servants are Dinah, the cook, and her husband, Sam Johnson, who is the gardener for the family.

The children have had many interesting adventures, some of which have been written down. In the story just before this one, you may read of the wonderful things that happen to them in the great North Country. This story is called "The Bobbsey Twins in Eskimo Land."

Now let us return to Daddy Bobbsey and his big surprise for the family, the brand new automobile. The twins continued to admire the car and to beg their father to tell them about taking them for a trip. Daddy Bobbsey refused to be pinned down to any definite promise, however. All he would say was:

"We may take a trip soon, but I'm not sure. Meanwhile," tactfully changing the subject, "is there any one around here who would care to go for a ride? If so, pile in and we'll take a little trip right now—around the block."

The next few days were filled with fun for the Bobbsey twins. All their little friends from the neighborhood, including Grace Lavine, John Marsh, little Susie Larker and Ted Blake came to admire the new car and to watch old Sam as he tried to learn to drive it.

Mr. Bobbsey hoped to make a very good chauffeur of the colored man. However, as they watched the old fellow fumble helplessly with the gear-shift, step on the starter when he should use the brake, and stall the engine whenever he wanted to speed it up, the children felt quite sure that the twins' father would never get his wish.

This belief was shared also by Sam's wife Dinah, who kept the twins and their friends in stitches of laughter with her comments on poor Sam's progress. "Ah jest knows he's gwine bust his head," she would usually say and waddle back into the house.

One morning at breakfast Daddy Bobbsey said that a very good friend of his named Mr. Ken Speer would come that evening to visit them. "He's a famous playwright," the twins' father added, as he said good-bye to his family and went to his office.

"What's a playwright?" Flossie asked Freddie when she and her brother were alone a little later.

"Golly, I don't know," Freddie confessed. "It's a funny sort of name, isn't it?"

Flossie looked thoughtful for a moment; then her face brightened.

"Freddie, do you remember that toy store we

pass sometimes when we go downtown?" she demanded. "The one that has 'Play Rite' over the door?"

Freddie nodded. "Play Rite," he repeated soberly. "That's what Daddy said Mr. Speer was. Say, Flossie," he said excitedly, "do you think Mr. Speer might have something to do with a toy shop?"

"He might," said Flossie a little doubtfully. "Anyway, I guess we had better have our toys ready to show him when he comes tonight. He may be interested to see them."

So it came about that when Mr. Speer, the famous playwright, entered the Bobbsey front door that evening he was greeted by a plump, fair-haired little girl and a sturdy, light-haired little boy. In their arms, gripped tight by chubby fists, were toys of all sorts, sizes and descriptions. As soon as introductions were over the visitor looked at Freddie and Flossie.

"Oho, what's this?" he asked, kneeling down so that he might put an arm about each of the twins. "I never saw so many toys—and nice ones, too. Where did you get them all?"

"Some of them came from the Play Rite shop," said Freddie.

"Have you many toys at your store, Mr. Speer?" asked Flossie eagerly.

"At my store?" repeated Mr. Speer, a puzzled look on his face. He turned to Mr. and Mrs. Bobbsey for help. "Why, I—"

"Daddy said you were a playwright," Flossie explained.

"And the only Play Rite we know is a toy shop, you see," Freddie explained.

Everyone laughed at this, and Mrs. Bobbsey told her little boy and girl as gently as she could that Mr. Speer's kind of playwright had nothing to do with toy shops.

"He writes plays," she concluded. "Very fine and successful plays which are acted on the stage."

"Oh, Mr. Speer," said Flossie with an excited bounce and skip, "will you please write a play for us? Will you?"

"Oh, please write a play for us, Mr. Speer," Freddie added pleadingly. "It would be lots of fun, and maybe we could even act in it."

"On the stage," added Flossie.

Mr. Speer laughed heartily and said that he thought it ought to be easy to write a play for the Bobbsey twins.

"Two pair of twins in one family give me all sorts of ideas," he said.

"Then will it be about us?" asked Nan eagerly. "A whole play about the Bobbsey twins?"

CHAPTER III

THE PLAY

"WOULD you like a play written just about yourselves?" Mr. Speer asked the Bobbsey twins. "Or one about other people but arranged so you four could act all the parts?"

Bert and Nan were not sure, but Freddie was. "I want both," he replied.

Mr. Speer laughed. "You're giving me a pretty big order, little man," he said. "I'll see what I can do, though—on one condition."

"What's that?" asked Bert.

"That you all will help me," he answered. "I can't think out a plot alone. You will have to give me some ideas."

"Oh, we have lots of those," said Flossie, looking very important. "We can give you all sorts of ideas, Mr. Ken Speer. Don't you worry."

Daddy Bobbsey laughed and ruffled Flossie's fair curls. "Come along, fat fairy," he said fondly. "Time enough after dinner to tell us

17

about all those wonderful ideas. Meanwhile, how about giving our guest something to eat?"

Flossie agreed that this might be a good idea, too. "I s'pose we can *think* about the play," she said quietly, "even if we can't *talk* about it."

But they did speak of the play at dinner in spite of Flossie's good resolutions. Mr. Ken Speer was deeply interested in the children and led them on to speak about their hopes and fears, their likes and dislikes, to find out more about them.

He listened to Freddie's and Flossie's ideas for a plot without cracking a smile, though he must have been very much amused at times, especially when the little boy said:

"I could be a fireman. I have a suit and an engine."

Mr. Speer heard with genuine pleasure some suggestions put forward by Nan and Bert which they thought might serve as a fine background for the plot.

"We were on a ranch once, so I know something about cowboys," said Bert, who felt rather proud because he had been to several far-away places.

However, it was not until Nan told about finding the diamond ring that the playwright really began to grow seriously interested.

"Now that's the kernel of a good plot for a

mystery play," he said. "Mysterious stranger stops in one afternoon, asks for a telephone book, strips off her gloves to look up a number, finds the number and goes away. Shortly after she has left a beautiful diamond ring is found on the floor."

"And no one knows who the strange lady is nor where she has gone to," Nan added eagerly.

"Exactly! And there you have the mystery. Who was the strange woman, how did she lose her ring—if it is hers—and why has she not returned for it?"

"And can you make all that into a play?" asked Freddie in an awed voice.

"Can we!" returned the pleasant writer, smiling. "I should say we can, young man. This will be a real corking good play, with lots of punch and snap to it."

"As—as good as the ones Flossie Fair acts in?" asked Flossie Bobbsey. "I hear her on the radio sometimes. She is my favorite star."

"You mean that little girl who speaks and sings?" Mr. Speer asked. "To tell you the truth, I've never heard her on a single program. When is she on the air? Maybe I should listen to her."

"She hasn't been on the radio in several weeks," replied Nan. "The program she acted in ended for the season."

"She's going to start again soon," added Flossie. "Oh, it must be fun to do that."

"Yes, it is," agreed Mr. Speer. "But a lot of work, too. Who can tell now, maybe one of you Bobbsey twins will be broadcasting some day, and make a great big hit with the listeners all over the world!"

"In the meantime," laughed Mrs. Bobbsey, "you children had better be content acting in plays at home. I'm sure the one Mr. Speer is going to write for you will be enjoyed by your family and friends. That will be a big enough audience for you to start with when you're doing it all alone."

Of course, the twins agreed with this, and promised to help in every way they possibly could. When they went to bed some time later they were still discussing the splendid idea of the play.

"I wonder how soon Mr. Speer will start it," thought Bert as he dozed off. "I hope soon, because I can hardly wait to see what it will be like. And then, we'll have a lot of fun play-acting."

The next morning Mrs. Bobbsey said that since the playwright intended to make them a fairly long visit, and the day happened to be free for Daddy Bobbsey, she thought it would be nice for the whole family to take a lunch and go out to the lake and have a picnic. The twins thought this would be lots of fun.

Soon the group, accompanied by a large hamper of delicious smelling lunch and some bulky fishing tackle, was on its way to the picnic grounds. As it was necessary for them to pass through Lakeview to get there, Nan suggested that they stop for a moment at the Hayman house to see if they could get in touch with the woman who had lost the diamond ring.

When they turned into the street where the Haymans lived they found signs of life about the hitherto deserted house. A wash was flapping on clotheslines in the back yard, while shades were raised and windows stood open.

"I hope we can find out about that woman who came to our house," said Nan thoughtfully, as she and her mother got out of the car and went to the front door.

"Of course, it's possible these people do not know her," returned her mother.

Just then the door was opened by a tall, heavily-built woman.

"Is Mrs. Hayman at home?" asked Mrs. Bobbsey.

"I'm Mrs. Hayman," the woman replied.

"We've come to ask about a young lady who stopped at our house by mistake a few days ago. She was looking for you."

"I've been away," said Mrs. Hayman, "so I

can't help you. Lots of people try to sell things, so probably the young woman you mean was here for that reason."

"I don't know about that," said Mrs. Bobbsey, "but we think she dropped a valuable piece of jewelry, and we should like to return it to her."

"Oh," said Mrs. Hayman. "Well, maybe I do know her. Won't you come in?"

She opened the door, took her callers into a small front room, and asked them to be seated.

"Now," she said, "will you please describe this person who, you say, called on you the other day and was so eager to find my house?"

Mrs. Bobbsey turned to Nan. "You saw the young woman, dear," she told her daughter. "Try to describe her as carefully as you possibly can so that Mrs. Hayman can get an idea as to what she looks like."

"She was very pretty," Nan began earnestly. "She had reddish-gold hair, and I think her eyes were blue—or gray, I'm not sure which. Her skin was very white, and she had such pretty hands, all covered with rings."

"How tall was she?" Mrs. Hayman's face had flushed and she was watching Nan closely.

"About Mother's height, I think," said the girl, hesitating. "Maybe she was a bit taller, though I don't believe so."

"Do you recognize her from the description?" asked Mrs. Bobbsey.

Mrs. Hayman had fallen back in her chair. Now she nodded vaguely, as though her thoughts were a long way off.

"I had a sister once," she said slowly. "She was much younger than I was and pretty—very, very pretty. When she was barely fifteen she ran away from home to go on the stage. We have never heard from her since."

"And you think this young woman who stopped at our door might have been your sister?" asked Mrs. Bobbsey gently.

"She may have been. She had reddish-gold hair and very beautiful eyes. They were deep blue. Her hands were long and slim with lovely tapering fingers. And to think," Mrs. Hayman sat up suddenly, while a spot of angry color glowed in her face, "that at the very time she tried to find me I was away from home and the house was all closed up. Isn't that just the way things happen?"

"No doubt if your sister tried to find you once she will come back again," said Mrs. Bobbsey in an attempt to comfort Mrs. Hayman. "If she should," she added, rising and drawing Nan with her toward the door, "please let us know. We shall be glad to give her ring back to her."

As the Bobbseys drove on toward the lake Nan

repeated the conversation with Mrs. Hayman. Ken Speer greeted this new turn to the "diamond ring mystery" eagerly.

"More ideas for the play," he said gaily. "This plot is going to be good, very good."

Before the twins could ask any questions Mr. Bobbsey had swung into a bumpy road leading to the lake, and soon the car reached the picnic spot.

"All out!" he called, and the joyful children scrambled from the auto.

"Gee, we're going to have fun," cried Freddie, running toward the water.

Mr. Bobbsey, Ken Speer, Bert and Freddie decided to fish in a cove. Since this type of sport was not attractive to the girls, Nan and Flossie wandered off in search of other amusement.

They had not gone far when they came upon an old rowboat, half hidden among the bushes on the shore of the lake. There were oars in it as well as a couple of old rusty tins which very likely had contained fishing bait once upon a time.

"I wonder if the boat is safe," said Nan.

"Let's take a ride," suggested Flossie.

She climbed in, and Nan shoved the craft down the shelving bank into the water. The little girl gave a squeak of pleasure as her sister jumped into the boat and took up the oars.

"We won't go far," said Nan, as she skirted the bushes on the bank and pulled out toward the center of the lake. "I'm not used to rowing and I'll probably get blisters on my hands."

"Ooh, but it's fun," cried Flossie, hugging her small, fat self. "We can make b'lieve we're going on a long, long trip, Nan. Across the ocean, maybe."

It was some time later that the older sister, resting on her oars, chanced to see something that made her heart beat a little faster. Water was seeping into the boat through its old, strained seams. The planks at the bottom were already awash.

"Oh, what shall I do?" Nan thought excitedly.

She glanced hastily toward the shore and saw that she had gone much farther from it than she had intended. She and Flossie were almost in the middle of the lake in a leaky old boat that threatened to sink at any moment!

CHAPTER IV

THE LEAKY BOAT

WITH a desperate sweep of her right oar Nan turned the boat about and headed toward shore. Her one thought was to keep little Flossie from realizing their danger as long as possible. Nan was a good swimmer but Flossie could keep up only a little distance.

"She could never get to shore alone," thought Nan with fast beating heart.

She pulled as hard as she could on her oars, pausing every now and then to glance over her shoulder and measure the distance to the shore.

"What are you looking at, Nan?" Flossie asked innocently. "Do you see Daddy and Mother and Mr. Speer anywhere?"

"I think they are just beyond that clump of trees over there," said her sister, pointing with one oar. "I can see the smoke from their camp fire."

To herself Nan thought anxiously, "I wish

26

Daddy would spot us. Oh, dear, there isn't anybody in sight anywhere. What will I do!"

Poor Nan's hands were getting blistered with the rubbing of the oars against the palms, and her back ached painfully. Still the water kept seeping into the boat more and more rapidly as the old seams opened wider.

Suddenly Flossie cried out in fright. "Nan, there's water in the bottom of the boat," she wailed. "And my feet are getting all wet."

The older Bobbsey girl sent a desperate glance shoreward. The boat was drawing nearer, though not near enough. It would sink before they could reach land. It was sinking now!

"Everything's all right, Flossie." Nan tried to speak calmly as a big sister should. "I—I'm afraid the boat is going to sink, and we can't reach shore in time. But everything will be all right if you will be a good, brave girl and do just as I tell you to."

"Y-yes," Flossie whimpered. "I'll try."

"Then come here." Nan caught the child as she floundered toward her. At the same time the seams of the old craft opened and the water poured in.

"Put your hand on my shoulder," gasped Nan. "We'll have to swim for it!"

Flossie clung to her sister's shoulder for dear

life, kicking furiously with her little feet as she had so often seen her daddy do.

"That's right," encouraged Nan, striking out as hard as she could for shore. "Just hang on, Flossie, and we'll—make it."

Nan swam on for what seemed to her a long, long time. After a while she grew so tired that it was hard for her even to lift her head and look toward the shore to see if it were any closer.

She did not hear her father's shout nor notice Mr. Bobbsey when he plunged into the water and swam in long, swift strokes toward the two girls. She was so tired that it was hard to remember to keep on striking out with her arms and kicking with her feet. She was so dreadfully tired—

"I—₁ can't do any more," she thought.

Just then Nan's knee struck something hard. She looked down and saw bits of jagged rock and a bed of pebbles right below her. She had brought Flossie into shallow water!

As she struggled to her feet with her little sister still clinging to her, Nan felt herself swept up into strong arms and heard a voice she scarcely recognized as being Daddy Bobbsey's saying over and over:

"My brave, brave little girl! Are you all right, Nan? Flossie, baby, don't hug me so tight. You'll choke Daddy."

Mr. Bobbsey carried them both to the camp, although Nan said that she was strong enough to walk. And what rejoicing there was when they reached the rest of the party, and what a lot of fuss was made over the girls.

Everyone said that Nan had been a real heroine. Flossie also came in for her share of praise for remembering to do just what her sister had told her to. She had not become frightened or panicky as people much older than Flossie sometimes do in the same predicament.

The girls were wrapped in blankets while their clothes dried in front of the fire. Then they were given broth to drink and hot hamburger sandwiches to eat until, between the warmth of the fire and the hot food, they began to feel rested.

After lunch the men folks—and these included little Freddie as well as Bert, of course—settled down in earnest to an afternoon of fishing. Ken Speer and Mr. Bobbsey had fairly good luck. By mid-afternoon there were several good-sized trout in the basket, besides one large catfish which Bert had caught and insisted upon keeping.

"I know real fishermen don't think much of catfish," he said. "But all the other fish I've caught this afternoon have been so small I've had to throw them back again. This fellow looks hefty, anyway."

Fish were not all that they brought up on their lines. The boys hauled in, among other things, a couple of old tin cans, a length of tangled rope, and someone's old discolored pocket handkerchief.

"Looks like a big day for the Bobbsey family," laughed Daddy Bobbsey. "Hello there, Freddie," he added, looking at his younger son with interest. "Hooked a fish, have you?"

"I don't know," said the small boy doubtfully. "It kind of seems like a fish, only it feels stuck, Daddy."

"How do you expect a fish to feel?" asked Bert with big brother scorn. "Go on and *pull*, Freddie. Give it a good tug!"

Freddie said "Oof!" Then he gave a hard pull and suddenly sat down with a bang right on the bank. His feet flew up into the air and the "fish" came down and hit him right in the middle of the chest.

"Golly!" said Freddie, round-eyed. "It isn't a fish at all. It's just a pocketbook!"

"Oh, good!" said Bert. "Let's see if there's anything in it."

The catch on the handbag was too much for Freddie's chubby fingers to open. His brother opened it for him and inside they found a crumpled, very damp one-dollar bill.

"My, this is better than any fish," cried Freddie. "A whole one-dollar bill! I'm going to keep it."

"If there isn't any name in the pocketbook I guess it belongs to you," said Bert. "Isn't that right, Dad?"

"Yes, that's right," replied his father.

The fishermen went back to the rest of the group and Freddie showed his find. Then, as he joyfully pocketed the money, Mr. Ken Speer laughed and ruffled the little lad's already tousled hair.

"If I were to live with the Bobbsey family a few weeks," said the playwright, "I'd get enough material for plots to last me all the rest of my life."

"What about the play you are writing for us?" Nan asked eagerly. "Have you thought about it any more, Mr. Speer?"

"We—el, I've made a few notes on the subject," said the man good-naturedly. "Perhaps you would like to have me read them over."

The enthusiastic way in which the young Bobbseys replied left no doubt in his mind that they wanted to hear them. While Mrs. Bobbsey brought out the remainder of the picnic sandwiches and passed around cups of steaming hot coffee from one thermos bottle and milk from another, Mr. Ken Speer read aloud the notes he had made on which he expected to base the plot for the children's playlet.

"I b'lieve it will be the very nicest play anyone ever had," said Flossie loyally, and the others agreed.

Soon after this Mrs. Bobbsey said they had better start for home. As she and Nan were about to pack up the picnic baskets, Flossie suddenly looked up, gave a squeal of fright, and flung both arms about her mother's neck.

"There's a bear!" she cried in terror. "Over there, in those bushes. It looked right at me!"

CHAPTER V

A QUEER KIND OF BEAR

A BEAR!

Daddy Bobbsey jumped to his feet and caught up a stout stick that lay near by. Mr. Ken Speer and Bert got to their feet also, while Mrs. Bobbsey placed herself before the other children as though to ward off whatever danger threatened them from the woods.

Suddenly Bert laughed. "It isn't a bear; it's a goat! Look, you can see its horns!"

At this moment the animal, as though to show off its horns to even greater advantage, charged into the picnic group and began to gobble up a piece of chocolate cake which Bert had left on his plate.

"Here, you can't do that!" cried the boy, dashing toward the invader.

Now, either this particular goat did not like boys, or else he was angered at being disturbed in the midst of his feast. Be that as it may, he refused to give an inch of ground as Bert rushed

33

at him; instead, he dashed forward to the attack on his own account.

The girls screamed, Daddy Bobbsey and Mr. Speer shouted advice, and Freddie jumped about excitedly.

"Run, Bert! Run!" came the cry.

But the lad did not run, and the lowered head of the goat caught the boy fair and square. It butted him into the midst of the picnic cloth, where the lad sat down right on top of what was left of the chocolate cake!

Having put Bert in his place, the goat turned and calmly left the scene, refusing to be hurried even when Daddy Bobbsey hit it a smart blow with the end of his stick.

"Oh, wasn't it funny?" cried Flossie, and burst into laughter.

It was amusing as well as exciting for all save poor Bert. Nan and his sister giggled until the tears ran down their cheeks.

But Freddie was very grave. "I was going to have another piece of the chocolate cake," he said.

This remark sent even the grown-ups into spasms of merriment.

"Oh, yes, you can laugh, all right," said Bert sadly. "But I can tell you that where the goat butted me I'm pretty sore. And look at all this chocolate cake! Get it off me, someone, will you?"

After his mother had scraped the gooey mass from her son's clothes, she and Nan packed up the remainder of the sandwiches. The boys cleaned up the picnic grounds, and soon the Bobbseys were ready to start for home. Everyone voted the day a great success except Bert, who insisted that he didn't want to see another goat as long as he lived.

Mr. Speer stayed with the Bobbseys for several days, and before he left finished the play for the children called "The Runaway Ring." The youngsters were thrilled, promising their kind friend to practice the scenes faithfully and have it all ready to act for him when he should come again.

"We wish you could stay and help us rehearse," said Nan. "You know just how the parts should go."

The playwright smiled. "I'm sure your mother and father can help you," he replied. "And it will be more of a surprise to me to see it as a complete performance."

"When will you come back to see it?" demanded Flossie.

"I can't say now," Mr. Speer answered. "I have some work to do in New York. I wish all the Bobbseys would come there, I couldn't invite you to stay at my place because it's too small. But I could show you many interesting things that you've probably never seen before."

"Oh, let's go!" cried Freddie.

"Wait a minute. Wait a minute," laughed Mr. Bobbsey. "Taking a family of this size to that big city just now would be a big task."

"I'll be ready to keep my promise any time you come," said the playwright as he departed.

The day after Mr. Speer left it was rainy and cold—the very best kind of weather, the twins decided, to stay indoors and go over their parts in the play.

"Mother, you please read it to us," asked Bert. "Then it will be much easier for us all to learn."

"I'll be very glad to do that," replied Mrs. Bobbsey, and seated herself in a comfortable chair by a window in the living room.

Nan had to act two roles; one of herself as a twin to Bert, and the other as an aunt who had lost a valuable ring some years before. This relative had disappeared also, leaving no trace of her whereabouts.

Bert had two parts; one of himself as Nan's twin, the other as father of the entire family in which he was a son. How Freddie and Flossie laughed to hear their brother try to change his voice from his own natural one to a deep bass growl which was supposed to belong to the father!

"I think he is very good," said Nan, standing by her twin. "I know *I* couldn't change my voice like that."

Time was called for luncheon hour, but the twins went back to their work directly afterward. Mrs. Bobbsey had to go out, and could not help them this time, so Nan read the lines.

"What does Waggo have to do in the play?" asked Flossie, as Bert brought in their pet.

"He is supposed to dig up the diamond ring at the right time. But probably he won't do it," replied her brother. "Lately he won't even bark when I want him to."

"Maybe we'd better let him dig up the ring outdoors," Freddie suggested.

"Mother wouldn't like to have him scratch up her rug," Flossie added.

"Well, he really doesn't have to scratch it up, does he?" queried Bert. "He can pretend. Let's try him. Now Waggo," he began, "you see that bone under there."

Evidently Waggo couldn't. He knew there was no bone under the big armchair in the living room and he couldn't understand why Bert was forever telling him to dig there for it. Instead, he tried by friendly barks and tail wagging to lead his young master out into the garden where there really was a bone—right in that soft mound of dirt in the corner near the hedge. Poor Waggo! All his small doggie world was upset and he couldn't make head nor tail out of it.

"I'll even have to growl for Waggo in the play," said Bert. "I used to think that dog was smart, but I'm beginning to doubt it," he added disgustedly.

Waggo was not the only difficulty the young actors had to overcome. In the play, Freddie, Flossie, Nan and Bert were supposed to be motherless children. They were very poor and needed the help of the rich aunt who, as you may remember, had disappeared years before. Despite their best efforts they could not find the aunt nor she them, although she had been searching everywhere for them.

Some of these early scenes were quite sad. One opened with Flossie seated all by herself in a lonely room and crying as though her heart would break. Flossie would always start out very well in this scene, but after the first sob or two she would be sure to think of something comical and begin to giggle. All this, of course, would spoil everything completely.

Then there was the problem of Freddie, who insisted that the lines of the play be changed all around so that he could bring his fire engine into it. "The play just won't be any good without my fire engine," he said over and over again, as Nan and Bert tried to argue with him. "I couldn't have any *fun* without it."

During one of these discussions there was a terrific rattling and clanging outside, and a real fire engine dashed past the house. The shriek of the siren drew the children to the window where they peered out into the street.

"The fire must be pretty close by," said Bert. "I can see a lot of people running."

"I'd like to go, too," said Nan, turning from the window, "but I guess we'd better finish our rehearsal. Come on."

"Where's Freddie?" asked Flossie, when they were ready to start.

Where indeed was Freddie? The children called the little boy's name, and then searched the house, even looking under beds and in closets in case he might be hiding from them for a joke. But he was nowhere about.

"He probably went out," said Bert. "He'll be back."

But Freddie did not come back.

"Wherever could he have gone?" said Nan at last, after an hour had gone by.

"P'raps he followed the fire engines," Flossie suggested.

"But the fire is out," said Bert. "I heard the engines go back a long time ago."

"Then Freddie is lost!" wailed Flossie. "My brother Freddie is lost!"

CHAPTER VI

A LONG SEARCH

"WELL, come on, we'll have to find him," said Bert. "You better stay here, Flossie," he added, giving his little sister a gentle push toward the living room. "We may not find Freddie right away and it's getting dark. You stay at home."

But Flossie clung to Nan's hand. "I want to help find Freddie," she pleaded. "Please let me go."

There was no talking the little girl out of it.

"All right, then, only hold onto Nan and don't get lost, whatever you do. One missing in the family is bad enough," said big brother Bert.

Flossie promised not to get lost, and the three children went out into the street together. Which direction should they take to start their search?

"Maybe Freddie stopped in some place on his way back," Bert suggested.

"But where?" wailed Nan. "There are a dozen places where he might stop."

"Freddie had five cents this morning," Flossie

stated gravely. "He saved it from his 'lowance. Maybe he went to buy ice cream."

Joe Clancy, the young clerk who handed ice cream cones and sodas over the counter of Brand and Smith, Confectioners, was sympathetic when he heard the children's story but could give them no news of Freddie.

"He hasn't been in here today," said Joe. "If I see him anywhere I'll be sure to tell him you were looking for him."

"Thanks," said Nan, and the children walked out into the street again. "Now where?" she asked.

As she spoke the children spied three of their friends.

"There's Grace," cried Nan. "Maybe she knows where Freddie is."

The girl had not seen the little fellow, but John Marsh and Charlie Mason, who came up just then, declared they had spied the young Bobbsey boy down at the fire.

"I hope he didn't get hurt," said Charlie. "He tried to rush into the store and grab some toys."

"What do you mean?" exclaimed Nan excitedly. "Where was the fire? What store?"

"Oh, didn't you know?" said John. "Down at the Play Rite shop. Some of the little boys who ran after the engines got real excited and tried to go into the place."

"And some were hurt?" asked Bert, very much disturbed. "What happened?"

"I couldn't see very well," answered Charlie, "but I saw Freddie rush inside the store. Then I heard a fireman yell, 'Get those kids out of here. They'll get hurt.' In a few seconds some glass crashed."

"Oh, my goodness!" cried Nan, beside herself with fear. "We must find out at once about Freddie."

The children raced toward the burned toy store. Upon reaching it they inquired of everyone they saw whether or not he had seen Freddie. No one had, and the Bobbseys were just wondering what to do, when Nellie Parks came along.

"Hello, Nan," said the Bobbsey girl's chum. "Some fire, wasn't it? Your little brother certainly likes to be around when the engines are working, doesn't he?"

"Do you—know—where he is now?" gulped Nan.

"Well, not exactly," replied Nellie. "He ran down the street with some other boys after the fire was out."

"Then he didn't get hurt?" cried Flossie.

"Hurt?" asked Nellie. "He didn't get hurt as

far as I know. He looked all right when he was running along the sidewalk."

The Bobbseys were greatly relieved, but still they had to find Freddie. Bert stopped in a telephone booth to call up the children's house. Perhaps his brother had returned home.

"No, Bert, no," came Dinah's voice over the wire. "That lil' fellow's not here and your ma'll be plenty worried 'bout it when she gets back."

When the lad joined the group waiting for him outside, he suggested they look for Freddie at the soldiers' camp near the outskirts of the town.

"He's just about as interested in soldiers as he is in fire engines," stated Bert. "And I heard him say yesterday that he wanted to go over to see the camp some time."

The Bobbseys said good-bye to Nellie and hurried off. When they reached the encampment, a guard at the gate told them they could not go inside.

"We have to find my twin," spoke up Flossie.

"I'm sure she's not here," said the young man in uniform. "Haven't been any little girls around here all day."

"He's not a girl," spoke up Flossie indignantly. "He's Freddie."

The soldier laughed and said he was sorry he had made such a mistake.

"There haven't been any little boys here to-day either," he added. "So I guess you'll have to look for him somewhere else."

The children moved away, hardly knowing where to turn in their search. By this time Flossie was tired and frightened. She clung to Nan and began to cry.

"I don't want anything to happen to Freddie," she sobbed. " 'Course he's naughty sometimes, but I guess he can't help that. Dinah says Freddie was just born to make trouble, but I like him anyway. We have such lots of fun."

While Nan gently comforted the sobbing little girl, she and Bert tried to think of some other place where their brother might be. They had about decided to go home and report the loss to their parents when Flossie asked, as the tears rolled down her cheeks, why they didn't look in the firehouse.

"Maybe he followed the engines all the way b-back to their home," she said.

"I bet you're right," exclaimed Bert.

The children wasted no time getting to the fire-house. They ran most of the way, with Nan and Bert carrying Flossie between them in a seat they made of their clasped hands. The little girl clung to them, her chubby arms about their shoulders, and urged them to greater speed.

Sure enough, in the firehouse they found Freddie, a joyful and excited Freddie, who was being shown by a genial fireman just how much fun a small boy could have sliding down a greased pole, the way the fire-fighters do when the alarm bell rings and they happen to be on the second floor.

"Watch me!" he cried, when he spied his brother and sisters. "I can slide down better than a real fireman. Now watch!"

Nan, Bert and Flossie were too glad to see Freddie to scold him very much, although Nan did tell him on the way home how worried they had been and how they had gone all over town looking for him.

"We thought you were lost for good," Nan said. "You really were very naughty to run away like that, Freddie, and not tell us where you were going."

"I'm awfully sorry," said the little boy soberly. "I started for home after the fire was out. But then I thought I'd follow the engine. It went so fast I couldn't catch up with it. Then I saw the firehouse and stepped inside. The nice man showed me how to slide down the greased pole. Golly, it was fun! I guess I've just got to be a fireman when I grow up."

Fortunately neither Mother nor Daddy Bobbsey had reached home when the twins returned to the house, so it was not necessary to report Freddie's naughtiness to them. The little fellow was so grateful for this that he promised Nan and Bert never to run after fire engines again without first telling some one where he was going.

The very next day after this happened Daddy Bobbsey received a message from a client of his in New York asking him to come to that city on important matters of business. He told his family about it when he came home from his office.

"Must you go at once, Daddy?" Nan asked.

The twins' father laughed. "Not this very minute," he replied. "I'll have some dinner first with my family. In the meantime we might see about what clothes to pack for the trip."

No one noticed that Flossie had become very excited and had run upstairs by herself. The other children wanted to know if the whole family were going along.

"Won't you take us with you, Dad?" asked Bert.

"Not this time, Son," replied Mr. Bobbsey. "I'll have to run down on the train alone. This will be a business trip."

"Another time," promised Mrs. Bobbsey.

"I wish we could go," sighed Nan. "It would be wonderful to visit New York."

"Mr. Speer said he would show us lots of things," Freddie reminded his father.

"That's right, he did," agreed Mr. Bobbsey. "But I can't take you along with me this time."

At that moment Flossie came down the stairs, her coat and hat on. In her arms was her favorite doll.

"Flossie dear, what are you doing?" asked Mrs. Bobbsey.

"I'm all ready to go with Daddy," said the little girl confidently. "On his trip to New York, you know. And I thought Dolly might like to go, too."

Mother and Daddy Bobbsey both exchanged glances. Then Flossie's father put an arm about his little daughter and explained, as gently as he could, that he would have to take this trip alone.

"I'm very sorry," he added, as he kissed his little "fat fairy."

Flossie's lip began to quiver and she hid her face against her daddy's sleeve. "I want to go so much," she whispered. "You said you would take us some place in the new car."

"We'll plan for that another time," her daddy promised. "But not just now."

"Will you be back soon?" asked Freddie, who was almost as disappointed as was Flossie to find that he must remain at home.

"I don't know." For a moment Mr. Bobbsey was thoughtful, then he said briskly, "I tell you what I'll do. If I find I have to stay in New York more than a few days I'll send for the family. How does that suit you?"

CHAPTER VII

BERT'S ACCIDENT

THE next morning all four twins were at the door to say good-bye to Daddy Bobbsey, and not one of them forgot to remind him of his promise to send for the family if he should find it at all possible to do so. The house buzzed with excitement after he had gone.

"Do you s'pose we'll really go?" Freddie asked his mother half a dozen times.

"Would we see Mr. Speer and would he show us his studio?" Nan wanted to know. "It must be a very interesting place."

Mrs. Bobbsey laughed and said she really couldn't answer all the questions.

"We'll just have to wait and see," she replied. "And now, who remembers what important date is coming along soon?" she added.

The children were silent for a few seconds.

"Was it some battle in history?" ventured Bert.

"No," said Mrs. Bobbsey. "Guess again."

50

"Prob'ly something I never heard about," spoke up Freddie.

"You know this date very well," smiled his mother. "What month is this?"

"Oh, I know!" cried Nan. "Daddy's birthday. It's coming real soon."

"You're right," said Bert.

Flossie began to jump around. "Goodie, goodie," she cried. "We'll have fun on his birthday. Even if he couldn't take his whole family with him to New York," she said, "he's the best daddy in all the world."

"I think I know of something that would please him very much in the way of a present," said Mrs. Bobbsey.

"Please don't make us guess any more," pleaded Nan with a laugh.

"No, Mother," said Freddie. "Tell us what the present is."

"All right," said Mrs. Bobbsey, "why not practice your mystery play and know it so well by the time Daddy comes back that you can give a performance of it for him on his birthday?"

"Say, Mother, that is a grand idea," cried Bert enthusiastically. "We can begin rehearsing today!"

"Right now!" urged Freddie.

"And Mother, will you watch us and tell us

when we do things wrong?" Nan asked eagerly.

"I will try my best, dear," agreed Mrs. Bobbsey, pleased with the success of her suggestion, "although I am afraid I shall make a very poor stage manager."

"You will be elegant, Mother," said Flossie, using one of Dinah's favorite words, and climbing on the couch to give Mrs. Bobbsey a kiss.

There was some difficulty at the beginning of the rehearsal because Waggo could not be found to do his part. The children looked all over the neighborhood for him but could see no sign of the little fox terrier. Dinah suggested that they use old Snap, but this was immediately hooted down by the young actors.

"Snap would go to sleep in the middle of the most exciting scene," said Bert.

"Well, from all Ah've seen, dis Waggo ain't likely to do much better," said old Dinah, and then went back to her kitchen to finish the preparation of a fruit pudding.

At last, after more searching, Waggo was located in a neighbor's yard where he had treed a cat.

"You naughty, naughty dog," said Flossie. The Bobbsey pet, still barking furiously at the cat, was captured by Bert and brought back to the living room to take his part in the play.

"Now we'll start all over again," directed Nan. "Flossie, you pretend to cry."

Everything went along smoothly until the performance came to the place where Waggo was supposed to dig up the diamond ring.

"Come here," Bert coaxed the dog.

The lad got down on hands and knees to show Waggo what was expected of him. Moving backward quickly he bumped into a small table. Instantly it tipped.

"Look out!" Mrs. Bobbsey cried sharply, but her warning came too late.

Before any one could move to prevent it, an almost priceless blue vase slipped from the table top and crashed to the hardwood floor. Bert jumped to his feet and stared in consternation at the smashed object.

"Oh, Mother, I'm sorry!" he cried. "I didn't know I was so close to that table."

"It's too bad," said Mrs. Bobbsey. "That belonged to Great-grandmother Bobbsey. I suppose I shouldn't have left it in such a place."

"Do you think I could stick the pieces together?" asked Bert. "I have some good glue upstairs."

"Don't bother to go for the glue, Son. I am afraid this vase is broken beyond repair."

Tenderly Mrs. Bobbsey began to pick up the

pieces of her prized ornament and the children got down on their hands and knees to help her.

"I wish I could do something," said poor Bert, staring in a guilty way at the ruins. "Maybe I could buy you another vase, Mother. I guess I could make money enough if I should try hard enough."

Mrs. Bobbsey put an arm about her older son's shoulder. "That's the kind of spirit I like to see," she said. "Accidents will happen, and of course you didn't cause this one on purpose."

"How can I earn some money to buy a new vase for you, Mother?" Bert asked.

"I'll tell you," replied Mrs. Bobbsey. "You may help Sam. He is going to put down a new cement walk from the house to the garage. If you want to earn money that way, I will pay you exactly what I would give an outsider for a day's work."

Bert's face brightened. "Thanks, Mother," he said gratefully. "And I'll work as hard as any two day laborers. I promise."

Bert soon had a chance to prove his willingness to work, for the very next morning things began to happen which made Sam decide to start his job at once.

"Dis yeah's a fine dryin' day," he remarked to Dinah as the two servants were eating their breakfast in the kitchen. "Ah thinks I'll get to work."

"Yes, dat's a good idea, man, fo' you to get to work," replied his wife. "But what yo' mean, a good dryin' day? Yo' sound as if yo' 'spected to wash some clothes, and Ah knows yo' ain't gwine do dat!"

She chuckled so loudly that Bert, passing through the kitchen, stopped to ask what the joke was. Sam explained that this was a good day for drying, but he did not mean to dry clothes; he meant to dry the new walk he would lay.

"Oh, are the cement and the sand here?" asked Bert.

"They'll come directly," replied Sam. "Ah's spectin' 'em to be delivered any minute."

No sooner had he said this than a big truck arrived with the materials for the new walk. Freddie and Flossie spied it from a front window in the house and rushed outside at once. Now these young twins never meant to be naughty, but had a habit of being so. This time was no exception.

"Think I'll climb up there," said Freddie to himself.

While the driver was busy getting out his order book to make sure which bags he was to leave at the Bobbsey house, the little boy pulled himself up on the back of the truck. Perhaps he might help the man, he thought! So without asking permission he tugged at a large paper bag of cement. He managed to move it to the edge.

Then something happened. Without warning both the bag of cement and the little boy fell off the truck. The paper burst, the contents came out, and a shower of gray dust covered Freddie Bobbsey. The tumble did not hurt any part of the little fellow but his pride. However, he was a sorry looking sight. As he picked himself up he coughed and choked.

"Oh, you bad boy!" cried the driver, who had leaped down and was looking at the mess. "Your pa'll have to pay for this."

Flossie was too frightened to say a word, but rushed into the house to tell her mother what had happened. She called so loudly that everyone heard her, with the result that Mrs. Bobbsey, Nan, Bert, Dinah and Sam hurried outside.

"Oh, Mother," cried Freddie, "I didn't mean to spoil the cement."

Mrs. Bobbsey was annoyed, but when she saw how funny her little son looked she had to laugh.

"Freddie, Freddie," she said, "must you *always* get into trouble? Go right into the house and take a bath."

As the little twin disappeared Mrs. Bobbsey

spoke to the driver and finally everything was fixed up. Sam said he could use most of the cement that had spilled out.

"Ah'll get to work right away, Mis' Bobbsey," he said, "and shovel up dis stuff. Den Ah'll start de walk."

"I'll help," offered Bert. "Be back soon as I change my clothes," he called, as he hurried into the house to put on an old shirt and overalls.

The boy helped Sam manfully. All day long he worked, mixing and carrying the cement and smoothing the surface carefully with a flat trowel so that not a shadow of a ridge or lump would be left when the cement was dry.

By late afternoon a good part of the work was completed. Bert and Sam looked over the result of their labors with a feeling of pride.

"Dat dere walk looks mighty good to me," said the colored man, mopping his face with a red bandana. "You work fine too, Mist' Bert. He'p me most as good as a man kin do."

"It does look pretty nice," agreed Bert. "And now let's go in and get some dinner, Sam. I could eat a whole pie!"

"Yassir, Mist' Bert," agreed the colored man with a grin. "Ah'm jest a mite peckish myself. Yassir, Ah feel like Ah could eat mah weight in po'k chops."

Perhaps it was just as well for the peace **of** mind of Bert and Sam that they did not see Freddie come out of the house and look over the work. But it was certainly too bad that they did not see him mix some cement as he had seen them do, dip his trowel into it and begin to fix up the driveway in front of the garage.

Poor Bert! Poor Sam! What a terrible end there was going to be to a good day's work!

CHAPTER VIII

NAN'S DISCOVERY

THE next morning Nan picked up a newspaper while her mother and the other children were finishing their breakfasts.

"I want to look up the radio programs," she remarked, glancing over that section.

"Well, don't turn the machine on to that sappy orchestra leader with the whipped cream voice," growled Bert, and Flossie giggled.

Nan could take a teasing, and she could do some of it herself, too, so she said to her brother, "All right. But while I'm in the house please don't make me listen to those mountain boys who sing through their noses and play that waa-waa music without any tune to it."

"Ho! Ho!" roared Freddie. "Why, they're fun, Nan."

"I can see," laughed Mrs. Bobbsey, "that boys always stick together, and that girls usually don't like the same things their brothers do."

"Here's something we're all glad to hear," said

Nan, pointing to a news item. "Except Bert, maybe," she added, winking at her mother. "It says, 'Flossie Fair, the small blond child who has delighted radio audiences for a year, will return to the microphone soon in a new series of programs. The famous little girl is now in Europe, but will sail in a short time for the United States.' "

"Goodie," said Flossie Bobbsey. "I love to listen to Flossie Fair. She's very talted, isn't she, Mother?"

"You mean talented," replied Mrs. Bobbsey with a smile. "Yes, she is, dear. And just your age, too."

Suddenly Nan saw something in the newspaper that excited her. She thrust the sheet into her mother's hand.

"Do you see that lady?" she asked, pointing to the picture of a young woman with large, beautiful eyes and a sweet smile.

"Why yes, dear," said Mrs. Bobbsey, holding up the paper. "She has rather an attractive face, hasn't she?"

"That's what I thought—the day she came here," said Nan eagerly.

"The day she came here," Mrs. Bobbsey repeated, puzzled.

"Why, this is the photo of the woman," Nan

explained, still excited, "who stopped here that day to ask for the Haymans, and dropped her diamond ring—at least we *think* she dropped the diamond ring. Her name is Lila Lee."

"Nan, are you sure this is the same person?"

"Well, pretty sure," said Nan. "Anyway, it looks a lot like her, Mother."

"And the name is probably only her stage name," remarked Mrs. Bobbsey.

"Don't you think we ought to call up Mrs. Hayman and tell her about it?" asked Nan.

"Yes, only I think we'll drive over instead of telephoning," said Mrs. Bobbsey briskly. "A personal interview is always so much more satisfactory, and we'll take along the picture, too."

Nan liked this idea, and wasted no time in getting a hat and pocketbook for her mother, whom she followed out to the garage. What was Mrs. Bobbsey's surprise when she tried to open the doors of the building to find them tightly stuck!

"Why, someone has piled cement in front of them," cried Nan. "Look, Mother, there is a heap of it all the way along!"

Mrs. Bobbsey bent down to examine this strange looking mess.

"Whoever could have done such a thing!" she exclaimed. "Sam would know better and so would

Bert. Freddie," she called as the little boy came out the back door, "I want to see you about something a moment. Come here, please."

Perhaps at that instant Freddie's conscience began to trouble him. Possibly from his mother's look and tone he gathered that it would have been just as well if he had not yielded to a temptation late the previous afternoon to build a new approach to the garage. At any rate, he came forward slowly at his mother's command, dragging his chubby legs.

"Freddie," said Mrs. Bobbsey severely, pointing to the curious ridge of cement, "do you know anything about this?"

The little boy wriggled uncomfortably. He frowned, and kicked with one broad-toed shoe at a pebble in the grass.

"Yes," he said at last. "I put it there, Mother. I thought it would look pretty."

"You thought it would look pretty!" Mrs. Bobbsey raised both hands in a gesture of despair. "Freddie, Freddie, what shall I do with you! Don't you see that you have cemented the doors tight shut?"

"Golly, I'm sorry, Mother," said Freddie, his face very white. "I didn't think it would keep the doors from opening."

"Well, never mind. The thing to do now is to

chip this cement away so we can get the car out. Find Sam and Bert, Freddie, and ask them to come here."

The older Bobbsey boy and the colored man came running, both full of anxiety to learn what had happened. Bert was indignant, as he felt his little brother had spoiled the looks of the new walk, but Sam, with a negro's sense of humor, only chuckled good-naturedly.

"Seems lak you'd better not do no helpin' 'round here, Mast' Freddie," he said with a wide grin. "Fust thing you know, we'll be gettin' things undone faster'n we can do 'em!"

Freddie was very remorseful at the trouble he was making for everybody and set to work with a will to undo the mischief. Flossie, very much entertained, bent over to watch while her twin hacked away with a little hammer at the stubborn cement.

Suddenly the little girl straightened up with a cry of pain and clapped a chubby palm to her face. "Something got in my eye," she whispered. "Oh, Mother, it hurts, it hurts!"

"Don't rub your eye, dear. My, what will happen next?" said Mrs. Bobbsey as she dropped to her knees in front of her small daughter and took out a clean handkerchief. "Now open wide —that's right. I know it hurts, dear, but I have to see where the piece of stone went. Ah—there it is! Only a little piece to make all that trouble isn't it?" On the twisted corner of the square of linen Mrs. Bobbsey displayed the tiny particle of cement which she had brushed out. "Feel better now, dear?"

"Y-yes," said Flossie, adding politely, "Thank you very much, Mother."

At last the garage doors were opened and Mrs. Bobbsey was able to get the car out. When she and Nan reached Lakeview they were fortunate in finding Mrs. Hayman at home. The latter recognized her callers at once and did not attempt to hide her eagerness as she invited them into the house.

"Have you heard anything about my sister?" she demanded as soon as they were seated. "She has returned to your house, perhaps, to ask about the ring? Oh, please tell me at once if you have any news!"

"We scarcely know how much of what we have found out is news and how much guesswork," Mrs. Bobbsey confessed. "But we will tell you what we have discovered and leave it to you to draw your own conclusions."

At this point Nan produced the section of the morning paper which contained the picture of the radio singer. She explained that she had noted a marked resemblance between it and that of the woman who had stopped at their door by mistake.

Mrs. Hayman took the paper from Nan's hand and scanned the face closely.

"I don't know," she said at last. "My sister was so young when she left home—scarcely more than a child. This might be a likeness of her but it is hard to be sure after all these years. Of course, the name Lila Lee is probably the one she uses on the radio."

"Why not send a note to the company on whose program this woman appears?" Mrs. Bobbsey suggested. "Or, better still, you might write to her directly in care of the radio station. If she is your sister she will certainly be happy to get in touch with you."

"Please don't forget to ask Miss Lee in your letter whether she has lost a diamond ring," added Nan earnestly.

"I certainly won't forget that," Mrs. Hayman promised with a smile. "Thank you both for all the trouble you have taken in my behalf—and my sister's. I shall write at once to the radio station and will let you know as soon as I receive a reply to my letter."

On the return trip to Lakeport both Mrs. Bobbsey and Nan were unusually silent. The mother was thinking how sad it was that families must be broken up and their members lost to one another over a number of years. The daughter was busy with thoughts of the diamond ring, realizing that it was several days since she had looked at the precious trinket at the bottom of the pile of clean handkerchiefs in her bureau.

As soon as they reached home Nan ran directly to her room. She pulled open the drawer of her dresser, found her handkerchief box, and felt at the bottom of the pile.

There was no sign of the diamond ring!

Carefully Nan removed each handkerchief. One by one she shook out their folds, hoping against hope to hear the clink of the metal ring upon the dresser top.

At last each piece of linen had been examined thoroughly. No longer could there be any doubt of the dreadful truth. The diamond ring was gone!

CHAPTER IX

THE DIAMOND RING

Poor Nan was stunned. She sat down on the edge of her bed to think the situation over, but the more she thought the worse it seemed to become.

There was no doubt about the facts. The diamond ring which she had placed at the bottom of the handkerchief box had disappeared.

But how had that happened? One thing was certain; the ring could not have got out by itself. Some one must have taken it from the box deliberately. But who would do that, Nan wondered anxiously. Certainly no member of her own family.

The servants? The girl shook her head almost angrily at this supposition. She knew that Sam and Dinah could be trusted as well as any member of the family. "I'd just as soon accuse myself of taking it," she said aloud. "Oh, dear! Now what *am* I going to do!"

Mrs. Bobbsey, passing through the hall, paused and looked into her daughter's room.

"Why Nan, I thought I heard you speaking to some one," she said, glancing about curiously. "Are you alone?"

"Yes. I was talking to myself," Nan confessed. "Oh, Mother, something perfectly awful has happened. I've lost the diamond ring!"

"My dear, how is that possible?" exclaimed Mrs. Bobbsey. "I thought you said you had put it away very carefully."

"I had," cried the girl, half in tears. "I put it in this handkerchief box, Mother. I placed it at the very bottom and nobody knew it was here but myself."

"Could you have pulled the ring out by mistake with one of the handkerchiefs?" Mrs. Bobbsey asked.

"Oh, no, I'm sure I couldn't have."

"Well, now, there's no use worrying about it until we are quite sure the ring is lost," said the frightened girl's mother sensibly. "Perhaps it has fallen into one of your dresser drawers; or it may have rolled under a piece of furniture."

Talking in this cheerful fashion, Mrs. Bobbsey helped Nan to search the room thoroughly. Between them they turned out the contents of the bureau, shaking each article of clothing carefully to make sure the ring had not been caught in its folds. They looked under furniture, beneath the edges of rugs, even in Nan's bed, but it was not there. At last it became apparent, even to Mrs. Bobbsey, that the ring certainly was not in the girl's room.

"Well, there's still the rest of the house to search," she said practically. "Let's get Flossie and Freddie and Bert and we'll all get to work."

The little twins rallied to the call eagerly enough because they loved to search for anything. It also gave them a chance to upset things and cause lots of excitement and confusion everywhere.

"Maybe we'll find some other lost treasures," said Flossie.

Bert was truly sympathetic with Nan, for he could see how unhappy she was over the loss of the ring and how desperately determined she was to find it.

"Never mind, Sis," he consoled her. "We'll get it if we have to turn the house inside out."

This they almost did. Poor Dinah was shocked at the goings-on, and followed after the Bobbseys as if in the wake of a cyclone, trying, with little success, to restore order to the Bobbsey home.

"Lawsy me, I never did see such a mess," she grumbled. "All de chairs is tipped over an' all de rugs turned up an' only ole Dinah to set things straight again. Ooh, lawsy me, what is dat!"

"Dat" were two small, white-robed figures which sprang out at Dinah from the dark interior of the linen closet. Now these figures should have frightened the colored woman very much, for they hopped about and moaned in a very ghostly way, but the effect was spoiled by a joyful giggle inside of one of the sheets—a giggle that could belong to no one but Flossie Bobbsey.

"Oh, why do you always go and laugh!" cried Freddie, throwing off his white robe in disgust. "Just when we were getting Dinah good and scared, too."

"Were you really scared?" Flossie asked the colored woman with interest.

"Scared most out o' mah wits, honey," Dinah replied obligingly. "Don' know when I ever did see more ghos'lier ghos's in all mah life. Seems lak Ah'm still a-tremblin' all ober."

The twins were delighted and pranced off to the next room, where there were more dresser drawers to upset and another beautiful closet in which to rummage.

Though the search for the diamond ring was something of a lark for Freddie and Flossie, it certainly was a very different matter for poor Nan. She grew more and more depressed as time went on and finally gave vent to her feelings in a burst of tears.

"I knew we couldn't find it," she sobbed, burying her face against her mother's shoulder. "The ring is gone for good. Suppose that woman should come back and ask for it. What would I tell her?"

"You would tell her the truth, dear, of course," Mrs. Bobbsey answered. "You had the ring, you put it away in what you thought was a safe place, but in some mysterious manner it has disappeared. That's the truth. There's nothing else to tell her."

Nan raised a tear-stained face from her mother's shoulder.

"But suppose the woman doesn't believe we lost the ring," she said in a strained voice. "Suppose she thinks we—*took* it?"

"Nonsense!" said Mrs. Bobbsey just a little sharply. "She won't think anything of the kind. If worst comes to worst," she added, gently brushing Nan's hair back from her hot forehead, "we can always give the woman the value of her ring, you know—that is, if we are certain it really belongs to her."

"But that would cost a lot," said Nan forlornly.

All during the afternoon the hunt for the missing ring continued. Nan and Dinah even turned out all the rubbish in the cellar. The girl scanned every crumpled bit of paper, every envelope and piece of old rag with the closest attention—but all to no avail.

"Well, anyway, we do know where it isn't," she said at the end of the long quest. "This is dreadful, Dinah."

Her hands were grubby and her hair rumpled. The blue linen frock she had on was wrinkled and soiled. There were smudges on the tip of her nose and the point of her chin.

"You better go an' take a bath, honey," Dinah advised. "Fix yo'self up an' put on some clean clo'es. Everything's goin' to look better when yo's all tidied up."

Although Nan took Dinah's advice and came down to dinner an hour or so later looking very spic and span, she could not hide the shadows under her eyes nor the tired droop of her mouth.

Bert, on the other hand, was in the best of spirits. He and Sam had finished their work on the new walk. The last of the cement had been laid just before dinner.

"I have earned almost enough money to buy you a new vase, Mother," he said as a plate with a generous helping of meat, potatoes and vegetables was set in front of him. "Any time you want to pay this hired man he'll take you downtown and you can pick out a new vase—any one you want," he added.

Mrs. Bobbsey smiled at her son and said that she would be very glad to go whenever he should ask her. "I am sure you and Sam have done excellent work on the walk," she added. "I'm going out first thing in the morning to look it over."

But alas! What a surprise she and the other members of the family were going to have after breakfast. For during the early evening of the day when the walk was just finished, Waggo, the mischievous fox terrier, had danced back and forth on the still damp cement.

Soon the smooth surface had been covered with hundreds of footprints. Moreover, the little dog had sat down a few times to lick off the wet grit from his feet or to scratch himself. In these places there were deep depressions. All in all, the newly-made section of the walk was a sorry sight and would have to be given another coat of cement.

The morning dawned clear, and directly after a meal which included some of Dinah's special corn bread, Bert and his mother decided to go outside to view the work of himself and Sam. The lad followed Mrs. Bobbsey through the kitchen and opened the back door for her. A few seconds later the two reached the scene of ruin.

"Oh gee!" cried Bert. "Mother, this is terrible!"

"It is a shame, certainly," said Mrs. Bobbsey. "What dog could have done it?"

"Not Snap, I'm sure," replied Bert. "His feet would make larger prints."

"No, not Snap," agreed the boy's mother, who was almost as fond of the Bobbsey pet as were her children. "He's too much of a gentleman, anyway."

"I hate to think so, but I'm afraid Waggo is responsible," said Bert.

The fox terrier was called from the house and his footprints measured. They matched!

The young dog seemed to know that his playfulness had done some harm. He put his tail behind his legs and hung his head in a very sad fashion.

"Maybe when you get a little older, Waggo," said Mrs. Bobbsey, "you will know better than to do such things. Bert, tie him up."

As usual, Sam was good-natured about the whole affair and said it would not take long to put a new top on the walk.

"It's lucky fo' us we didn't use up all dat sand and cement," he chuckled. "Come on, Mist' Bert, let's get to work."

Mrs. Bobbsey watched for a few minutes as her son and the colored man got out the implements they had put away the afternoon before and started mixing a fresh batch of material for the walk. Bert went for a pail, and while filling it with water from the hose faucet at the side of the house he noticed the postman coming along the street.

"I hope there's a letter today from Dad," he said to himself. "I wonder how he is."

He had not long to wait to find out. By the time he had filled the pail and carried the water to the mixing trough where Sam was working, Flossie came running through the back door of the house. She was waving an envelope in her hand.

"Here's a letter!" she cried. "It's for you, Mother, and I think it's from Daddy. Maybe he wants us to come to New York! Oh, please hurry up and open it!"

CHAPTER X

BERT and Flossie stood in silence a few moments as their mother read the letter from Daddy Bobbsey. The children tried to guess from the expression on her face whether or not she was pleased at what she was reading.

"Oh, do hurry and tell us what it says," begged Flossie.

"Don't be so impatient, little sister," said Bert, who really was just as impatient as Flossie but was trying to act grown up.

Mrs. Bobbsey smiled. "I think it would not be fair to tell the news without Nan and Freddie hearing it at the same time."

"I'll get them," offered Flossie, running toward the house.

"We'll all go inside," suggested Mrs. Bobbsey, and started for the kitchen door.

In a few moments she and the twins gathered in the living room, and sections from the letter postmarked "New York" were read aloud. It

76

was not until Mrs. Bobbsey reached the last paragraph that the twins became really excited.

"As I find," wrote Daddy Bobbsey, "that I must stay here much longer than I had thought, I should like you and the children to come on as soon as possible. I am sure we shall have a glorious time together."

"Oh, we're really going!" cried Flossie, bouncing up and down on the sofa until the springs fairly rattled.

Freddie turned a somersault in the middle of the room and made queer noises to show his happy state of mind. They sounded something like caged animals which are about to receive a good meal.

"That's wonderful!" exclaimed Nan. "There are so many marvelous new things to see!"

"Mr. Speer promised to show us some of the sights," Bert reminded the others. "Gee, that'll be great! How soon can we go, Mother?"

Mrs. Bobbsey said there was a great deal to be done before they could start on the trip, but she thought that if the twins would do their share in the preparations the journey could begin on the day following the next one.

"Then the first thing I had better do is help Sam with the walk," said Bert, "because the wet cement has already been mixed and we don't want to waste it."

He ran from the house and at once told Sam the good news about the visit to New York.

"Dat's splendid," agreed the colored man. "You is lucky chilluns."

"You're right, Sam," said Bert, "we are lucky."

As the lad worked he whistled happily, and soon the job of repairing the walk by covering up the footprints Waggo had made was nearly complete. The older Bobbsey boy suddenly thought of a way to tease poor Sam.

"Better hurry up and get this job done, Sam," he said. "You will have to go with us to New York, you know."

"No sir, I ain't goin'," said the colored man, looking up in honest surprise. "What'd I do in N' York, I'd like to know? Ain't nothin' there but skyscrapers an' city streets. No sir, old Sam he's goin' t' stay right here."

"Well, then, who will drive the new car?" asked Bert, and then smiled at the sudden worried look on the man's face.

"You-all don't mean I got to drive de new car all de way to N' York!" he cried, his eyes as big as moons in his black face. "No sir, I ain't goin' to do it. Not old Sam!"

"Well then, I guess we'll just have to stay home," said Bert with a shrug of his shoulders. "Dad wouldn't want Mother to drive so far. And of course I can't do it because I'm not old enough," he added, hardly able to keep from laughing. "So I guess we'll have to stay home after all. Poor Daddy, he *will* be disappointed."

"Oh, lawsy me!" Old Sam mopped his perspiring brow and regarded his young tormentor sadly. "Looks like I got to drive dat car, an' no mistake."

"What worries you so much about it, Sam?" asked Bert.

"I didn't mind de old car," said the colored fellow, returning to his work on the driveway. "But dis new one's got too many gadgets. I don't hold wif so many ob dem things nohow. Ain't no sense to 'em. Gits you all mixed up tryin' to think which is which."

Bert began to feel sorry for Sam when he realized that the servant was really worried and that the teasing had gone almost too far. "Well, Sam, I'll see what I can do about it for you. Perhaps Mother will drive after all. I'll ask her."

"Oh, thank you, Mist' Bert," sighed the old servant. "Ah knows she'll do it. Ah'd like to see de big city, but not if Ah's got to git mah'self dere driving a car. By de way, Ah've been thinkin' you might buy somethin' for me while you are there."

"I'll be very glad to," offered Bert. "What is it?"

"Ah've been wantin' to git a nice present fo' Dinah," explained Sam, "and Ah think she'd 'preciate one from N' York. Ah wants to git a diamond ring. Not a cheap one like you buys in the five-and-ten cent stores, but a good one."

"How much do you want to spend?" asked Bert, knowing how expensive good diamond rings are.

"Well, seein' as how it's for Dinah, Ah thinks Ah'll spend a whole dollar on it."

Bert said he would be very glad to see what he could do while he was in the city, and Sam smiled contentedly.

"Ah means it to be a surprise for Dinah," he chuckled.

"I'll keep your secret," promised Bert, as he smoothed out the last section of the newly-made cement walk with a flat trowel.

While this conversation had been taking place, Nan and her mother had been talking over what clothes they should take with them to New York. It was found that several small articles would have to be bought, so the Bobbsey girl had offered to go downtown to do the shopping.

"Flossie should have a couple of pair of white socks, don't you think, Mother? She has several colored pair, and white ones look so nice with some of her dresses."

"You are right," said Mrs. Bobbsey. "Add those to your list. My, you have so many things to do I think perhaps you should see if one of your friends will go with you to help you."

Nan thought this was a good idea, and at once went to the telephone to call Grace Lavine. Her chum said she would be delighted to go along, and would meet Nan at a certain street corner in fifteen minutes.

"You must tell me all about what you are going to do in New York," said Grace just before hanging up the receiver.

Nan got her pocketbook and skipped down the stairway. She decided to stop in the kitchen a moment to get a cool drink of water and also to tell Dinah the news about the proposed stay in New York. The old colored woman was delighted at what she heard.

"Dat's mighty fine," she said, "and maybe you'll do something for me while you is dere, Nan. Dat man o' mine Sam has been telling me fo' years dat dere is one thing he's been hoping all his life to get, an' now maybe his chance has come."

Nan laughed. "What in the world could Sam want so much?"

Dinah chuckled. "You see, Sam's pappy had a lot to do wif horses, an' when he got dressed up he allus wore a red vest, an' my Sam has allus wanted a red vest like his pappy wore."

"I'll do my best, Dinah," promised Nan. "I never saw one myself, but probably one can buy everything in New York, so I will be glad to do your errand for you."

The colored woman was very pleased, and thanked Nan over and over. "I'd like to keep it a secret," she said seriously.

"I'll be sure to do that," said Nan as she left the kitchen and hurried toward the corner where she was to meet Grace.

Her chum was awaiting her. Arm in arm the two girls walked through the business section of Lakeport. Then Nan got the list from her pocket-book.

"Let's go into this children's shop first," she suggested. "I have to buy several things for Flossie."

For an hour the two girls went from store to store buying the needed articles, giggling over some of the amusing happenings, and doing a great deal of talking about the trip which the Bobbsey family was soon to take. At last the purchases were all made, and Nan invited her chum to go to an ice cream store for refreshments.

"It will be good to sit down," laughed Grace, "and I am thirsty. I am glad you mentioned it. Vanilla ice cream with chocolate sauce will taste very good just now."

Their arms loaded with bundles, the two girls hurried to the Brand and Smith Confectionery Store. As they were about to enter, Nan dropped one of her parcels. A woman directly behind her picked it up.

"Hello, it's Nan Bobbsey," she said, handing the girl the package. "I think you dropped this, my dear."

"Oh yes, thank you, Mrs. Hayman," Nan replied as she recognized the woman. She accepted the bundle and restored it to the pile under her arm. She paused a moment, wondering if she should speak about the lost diamond ring. Instead she said, "I've been wondering—at least Mother and I have been wondering—whether you have heard anything from the lady who had her picture in the paper. The radio singer, I mean."

Mrs. Hayman shook her head. "I have written to her but she has not answered me as yet. Well, good-bye, my dear," she added as she turned away. "Please remember me to your mother and tell her that I shall let her know as soon as I have word from the lady."

Nan thanked the woman in a faint voice and hurried inside the ice cream store with Grace.

"I should have said something about the diamond ring," she thought uneasily. "I guess I will write to Mrs. Hayman about it."

However, in spite of her good intentions, Nan did not write to Mrs. Hayman. She kept putting it off, partly because she hated to tell her she had lost it, and partly because she was really very busy helping her mother and Dinah get ready for the New York trip.

The next day sped by on wings, and when night came all the work had been done and the suitcases packed and safely locked in the roomy trunk compartment of the new car, ready for an early start the following day.

Next morning the Bobbsey family was up before any of their neighbors. The sun was shining brightly and everything looked to be favorable for a wonderful trip.

Freddie was the first one dressed. Unseen by anyone, he slipped outdoors. "I must do it," he said to himself. "I shan't have a good time in New York if I don't. Maybe I ought to ask permission, but I'm 'fraid Mother wouldn't understand. And I just have to do it."

The little fellow went toward the garage. Then he ran back to the house and disappeared in the cellar.

Meanwhile the other members of the family finished dressing, and by seven-thirty they were ready for breakfast. When they were about to sit down to the table, Mrs. Bobbsey asked where Freddie was. Dinah called out the name of the little boy, who finally came scurrying in from out-doors.

"I wonder where our next meal will be," said the twins' mother cheerily. "We ought to get a good distance from here by noon time. Why Freddie, what are you doing?" she added, as she saw her small son put a teaspoonful of sugar on his egg.

"Why—why," stammered Freddie, "I didn't realize it." He blushed furiously. "I guess I'm 'cited, Mother."

Mrs. Bobbsey thought no more about the matter for a few minutes. Then she noticed how shaky the little boy's hands were. When he spilled a whole glass of milk on the clean white cloth she became alarmed.

"Freddie," she said, "are you ill?"

"I'm all right, Mother."

"You're quite sure?" she asked, feeling of his forehead to see if perhaps he had a fever.

"Real sure," replied the little boy. "I'm just 'cited, I tell you."

At that moment the front doorbell rang. Dinah went to answer it and talked to someone for a few minutes before coming to the dining room.

"An early caller," remarked Mrs. Bobbsey. "I wonder who it can be?"

Then the old colored servant appeared and said, "There's a strange lady at the door wants to see you, Mis' Bobbsey, or else Nan. I told her you-all is goin' away and maybe she could come some other time."

"What did she say?" asked Nan, feeling a little frightened.

"She done say it's important," said Dinah. "She came to get a diamond ring!"

CHAPTER XI

A CONFESSION

Nan turned pale when she heard what Dinah said, and looked at her mother.

"Mrs. Hayman!" she cried with a catch in her voice.

"Maybe the caller is Miss Lila Lee," offered Bert.

"Oh, I hope the woman isn't either one," whispered Nan. "But of course she is," the girl added quickly, "for no one else knows about the diamond ring."

"Tell the woman to step into the living room, Dinah," said Mrs. Bobbsey.

"I don't have to see her, do I, Mother?" Nan stammered. "Can't *you* tell her about—about the diamond ring, and how I lost it? I just can't do it."

"Of course you can," said Mrs. Bobbsey, putting an arm about her daughter. "When an unpleasant situation has to be faced it is much better to face it at once and get it over. Come along, dear."

As Mrs. Bobbsey and Nan entered the living room their caller turned and came toward them eagerly. She was Mrs. Hayman!

"I have the best of news," the woman declared vigorously. "I have just had a letter from the radio singer and find that she *is* my long-lost sister."

"I am so glad for you that you have found her," said Mrs. Bobbsey, smiling.

"And I am, too," added Nan.

Mrs. Hayman rushed on. "In my letter I spoke to my sister about the ring and she says that she did lose one the day you mentioned. She describes the piece of jewelry, and I believe you will find the description entirely to your satisfaction. I have it right here," rummaging in her pocketbook and producing a letter. "You may read it yourself."

Mrs. Bobbsey carefully noted the description of the ring, then silently handed the letter to Nan, who also read it.

"A large white diamond in a square platinum setting," were the words poor Nan saw.

Her hands were shaking so much she could scarcely hold the note. It was not necessary for her to read any more. Without the shadow of a

doubt the ring belonged to Lila Lee; Lila Lee,
who was, strangely enough, Mrs. Hayman's sister. And Mrs. Hayman had come to claim her
sister's property!

How easy it would be, thought Nan miserably,
if she could go upstairs, take out her handkerchief box from the dresser drawer, find the ring
where she had hidden it beneath a pile of sweet-
smelling, freshly-laundered linen, and hand it to
Mrs. Hayman.

"You recognize the description of the ring,
don't you, dear?" asked Mrs. Bobbsey.

Nan nodded dumbly, and over the caller's face
there spread a look of satisfaction.

"I was hoping you would say that," she said,
taking the letter from Nan's unsteady hand and
returning it to her purse. "I know how glad my
sister will be to get back her property."

The speaker paused, and Nan, knowing that
the terrible moment was at hand, burst out:

"I haven't the ring, Mrs. Hayman! I'm dreadfully sorry, but—that day after Mother and I
had been to see you about Miss Lee's picture being in the paper I went up to look in my handkerchief case where I had put the ring and—it wasn't
there. It had—disappeared."

"Disappeared?" repeated Mrs. Hayman with
a deep frown. "I don't think I quite understand

If you put the ring away for safekeeping how could it possibly have disappeared?"

"I don't know," stammered Nan, tears springing to her eyes. "I couldn't understand it either, Mrs. Hayman. I *did* try to take good care of it, and I'm dreadfully, dreadfully sorry!"

"My sister may not understand," said Mrs. Hayman rather stiffly. "You may have to be prepared for something unpleasant when she hears of this."

"I believe we *are* prepared for just that thing," said Mrs. Bobbsey quietly. "As soon as we reach New York we will go directly to your sister and explain the situation to her. If, after a reasonable time, the ring is still missing, we will make her loss good in dollars and cents. That is fair enough, isn't it?"

Mrs. Hayman hesitated for a moment, then held out her hand with a smile.

"Entirely fair," she agreed. "And you, Nan, must not feel too bad," she added, patting the girl's shoulder, and then starting for the door. "Carelessness is common to youth and to older people as well. Perhaps the ring will turn up yet."

"I hope so," said Nan earnestly. "And I shan't stop looking for it until I find it, Mrs. Hayman, I promise you!"

"Now Nan, dear," said Mrs. Bobbsey, as soon as their caller had left, "we must get started. Run upstairs and bathe your eyes. You mustn't begin a nice trip with tears," she added with a smile.

Presently the children were ready, and the family gathered in the garden. Sam and Dinah had a great deal of advice to offer about the Bobbseys being careful.

"You all look out for dem New York taxi-cabs," warned Dinah. Then to Nan she whispered, "And don't forget dat red vest fo' Sam."

"I'll remember," promised the girl in a low tone.

Sam was shaking his curly gray head and saying, "You-all watch out when you goes underneath dat big city. I don't cotton much to ridin' under streets and under rivers, no sir." As the Bobbseys smiled, he added quietly in Bert's ear, "Be sure you pick out a extra special nice diamond ring fo' Dinah."

The lad assured the old servant he would do his best, and then helped his mother into the driver's seat of the car.

"All aboard!" sang out Freddie. "Toot! Toot! Too-oo-oot!"

In gay mood the twins and their mother started off, shouting good-byes to the colored couple who waved until the car was lost to view. Dinah wiped a tear from her eye, and said to Sam, "Dey's de bestest famil᠎ in de whole world, and don't tell me nothin' different. I'se goin' to miss 'em a heap."

"Huh," replied her husband, "I ain't likely to fuss wif yo' 'bout dat. I agrees wif yo'."

The Bobbsey car skimmed along the road. The children talked about the new auto and decided that it was very fine.

"There's just one thing missing," said Bert. "A radio would make it complete."

"That's right," agreed Flossie. "If we had one, then sometimes when we're out, and I want to listen to Flossie Fair, I might do it."

Mrs. Bobbsey laughed. "You children should be satisfied with what we have," she chided them. "Anyway, the little star you speak of won't be on the air for a while yet, so you probably won't miss her, Flossie. By the time we get home again, you can hear her on our own radio, and—why, what's that noise?" she asked suddenly.

"Sounded like a dog," said Flossie.

A loud whining was repeated.

"What is that?" Mrs. Bobbsey demanded again. "Certainly we have no dog in the car with us."

"It's probably Bert practicing Waggo's part in our play," suggested Nan.

"That shows that even a twin sister can be wrong once in a while," Bert retorted. "I haven't opened my mouth for the past five minutes."

"There it is again! It surely sounds like a dog whining!" exclaimed Mrs. Bobbsey. She drew up to the side of the road while both sets of twins got out of the car to look about them.

"Perhaps the noise we heard was air slowly going out of one of the tires," Bert suggested, walking around the auto.

However, the tires were all right. Mrs. Bobbsey, considerably mystified, was about to drive on again when the whining started once more. This time it was unmistakable—the frantic whining of a dog, coming, of all places, from the trunk compartment at the rear of the car!

"Let me have the key, Mother, and we'll soon solve the mystery," said Bert.

When the compartment was opened, what should come tumbling out of it but a very rumpled and sad looking fox terrier. Even in his sorry state he could be identified without any trouble as Waggo, the family pet!

CHAPTER XII

A PROBLEM

"WELL, I'd like to know how *you* got here," said Mrs. Bobbsey, regarding poor Waggo with disfavor.

As she turned to look at the children, she caught the guilty eye of Freddie, who hung his head and stubbed his toe in the dirt of the road.

"I put Waggo in the trunk compartment, Mother," he confessed. "He wanted to go along on our trip so I thought maybe it wouldn't do any harm to bring him."

"But Freddie, we can't take a dog to the city," said Mrs. Bobbsey. "Besides, he might have smothered to death. Well, the only thing to do now," she added, "is to stop at some nice farmhouse and see if the people there will keep Waggo for us until we come back."

At the first place they reached the kindly owner and his pleasant-faced wife promised to take care of the pet. Mrs. Bobbsey said she would pay them for their work.

Waggo, unfortunately, wanted to start making trouble right away. With an excited bark he pounced on a prize hen belonging to the farmer and had to be hauled away from the indignant fowl by sheer force. The farmer became angry, and decided he would not board the fox terrier.

The Bobbseys and Waggo went on again until they came to another farm where a man with a three-day-old growth of beard on his chin promised to take good care of the animal. After the travelers had tied up the pet and started on their way again, the poor dog's howls of distress followed them pitifully.

"Oh, can't we please go back?" begged Freddie, almost in tears.

"I guess we'll have to," said Mrs. Bobbsey. "I haven't the heart to leave him."

She turned the car around and drove to the farmhouse. Waggo shook his tail so hard that Flossie was afraid he was going to shake it off.

"I'm glad we're going to take him," said Nan. "I'm sure that man wouldn't have been kind to him."

After that Waggo rode with the family. He shared in the picnic lunch they ate along the road, and at night, when they stopped at a pleasant tourist camp, it was agreed that he would sleep in a room to be shared by Freddie and Bert.

While Mrs. Bobbsey completed arrangements with the husband and wife who owned the place, Flossie slipped away by herself to explore her new surroundings. She loved tourist cabins, she decided, especially the little ones, because it seemed to her that they were just like overgrown doll houses. She wished again, as she had often done before, that Mother and Daddy Bobbsey would build one for her in the garden of their home at Lakeport.

What fun it would be, she thought, to invite all the little girls of the neighborhood to her very own house to tea!

As Flossie walked beyond the place where the cars were parked, and went down a little hill at the back of the camp, she came to the dearest little cabin she had ever seen. It was like a doll house. Although it contained accommodations for only one person, it was complete in every detail, even to the tiny porch, on which stood a comfortable rocking chair. The little girl sat down in the seat and for several moments rocked contentedly back and forth while she gazed at the landscape.

"I'd like to make believe I live here all by myself," the little twin thought. "I b'lieve it might be fun to stay all alone, at least for a while."

When she grew tired of rocking Flossie went

inside the cabin and closed the door. There was a key in the lock on the inside. This she twisted until she heard a click. Then she looked around, and finally tried the bed, just as Goldilocks must have done. At last she decided it was time to leave. But she could not turn the key!

"My goodness, I wonder if I've locked myself in," thought the little girl. She tried the knob and pulled hard but the door held fast. "Oh, dear, I *have* locked myself in," she cried a little fearfully. "I hope somebody finds me pretty soon, 'cause it won't be much fun to be shut up here all by myself after dark."

This idea was so alarming to Flossie that she set to work on the lock again with renewed energy. She tried with all the strength of her chubby hands to turn the key, twisting it this way and that. She rattled the knob frantically, but still the door would not open.

Meanwhile the other Bobbseys were busy unpacking their luggage and carrying it to their sleeping quarters. For some time no one missed Flossie. Then Bert, who wanted to ask his little sister a question, discovered that she was not in sight.

"I better look for her before Mother realizes she's gone," he thought. "Gee, I hope she isn't lost."

He searched around, calling Flossie's name softly. There was no answer. He looked around the main cabins, in the car, and through a patch of woods. Still he did not find her.

Finally he spied the tiny cottage at the back of the camp. He hurried toward it and again called his small sister's name.

"Flossie! Flossie!"

The little girl inside the building was on the verge of tears, when she heard the voice outside. She listened closely, and with great joy recognized it as that of her brother. In another moment she was saying:

"Bert, I'm in here!" She shouted as loudly as she could. She began banging on the door with both her chubby fists. "I locked myself in and I can't get out!" she cried.

For a moment there was silence outside. Then Flossie could tell by the sounds of hurrying feet that her brother had heard her and was running toward the cabin.

"Flossie, are you all right?" he called from just outside the door.

"I'm all right," she answered sturdily. "But I turned the key in the lock and now I can't get out."

"Well, try again," her brother said urgently. "But be careful not to bend or break the key."

"I'm afraid I've bent it already," said Flossie unhappily. "I can't turn it at all, Bert. I've tried and tried."

The lad pushed on the door, turned the outside knob and did everything he could think of to help the key open the lock. But nothing did any good.

"Try the window," said Bert finally. "Maybe you can open that."

"All right," said Flossie.

But the cabin's only window was set high up in a wall, far too high for Flossie to reach even while standing on her toes.

"Get up on a chair," her brother directed anxiously. "But don't fall, whatever you do."

Even with the aid of the chair, which was not very steady, Flossie was unable to open the window. She strained and pushed until she was out of breath, but still the window refused to budge.

"Oh, dear, maybe I'll have to stay here all the rest of my life," sobbed Flossie, "like the princess in the enchanted castle. Only I'm not a princess and this isn't an enchanted castle and—oh, I do wish you would get me out!"

She began to drum on the door with her fists.

"I want to get out of here," she cried. "It's getting dark and I don't care to stay in here any longer."

"Don't be frightened," Bert's voice came to

her. "I've thought of a plan. You wait a minute. I'll have you out in a jiffy," he added.

Flossie heard her brother go away. She could tell by the sound of his retreating footsteps that he was leaving her. For what seemed to her an age she sat alone in the dark cabin, her chubby hands clasped tightly in her lap and her ears straining for the sound of his return.

Presently she heard the crunch of wheels. A car was coming slowly down the bumpy road. At first Flossie had the wild idea that Bert hoped to free her by running the auto into the cabin. With this thought in mind she got as far from the door as she could get.

Then she heard the car stop at the side of the little house directly beneath the window. A brake was pulled on.

There was a brief silence for several seconds. The next moment, to Flossie's great delight, Bert's face appeared at the window.

"Hello, there," he said. "I told you I'd get you out."

He grinned at his little sister as he thrust up the sash and jumped into the room.

"How—how did you do it?" Flossie gasped, as she rushed to him and flung her arms about him gratefully.

"Oh, easy," he said. "Our car was right at the

top of this hill. So I got into it, let the brake off, and coasted down here right under the window. I climbed on top of the auto, and—here I am."

"I'm so glad," said Flossie fervently. "I've never wanted to be a princess anyway, and I always thought it must be terrible to have to live in an enchanted castle," she added as Bert lifted her in his arms and thrust her through the window.

Everybody was glad to get Flossie back, for by this time the others had missed her, too. Even little Waggo was happy, and made the echoes ring with his frantic barks.

The Bobbseys were tired after the long trip, so as soon as they had eaten a plain but plentiful dinner at the house of the camp owners, they went directly to the large, rambling cottage which had been assigned to their use for the night.

Early the next morning they were on their way again. Waggo was left behind with the couple who owned the camp. Long after the Bobbsey car disappeared down the road the little dog's plaintive barks of protest still followed it.

Freddie was wistful for some time after they had left the tourist camp, for he hated leaving his pet behind. He cheered up considerably, however, at the thought that the people would take excellent care of the dog. Also, he was going to meet Daddy Bobbsey!

"What time will we get to the city?" Nan asked her mother when they had been on the road for an hour or two.

"If all goes well, we should be there by noon," said Mrs. Bobbsey cheerfully. "Perhaps in time to have lunch with your daddy," she added.

By twelve o'clock they actually had reached the city and soon were caught in the heavy traffic that makes driving so difficult.

Once Nan said to Bert, "I'm glad Mother is driving instead of Sam, aren't you?"

"Poor old Sam," laughed her brother. "I bet he would have been frightened to death long before this. But Mother drives like an expert," he added admiringly.

A few minutes before one o'clock Mrs. Bobbsey drove up to the hotel at which her husband was staying. A polite doorman promised to take care of the car for them, while porters in the most perfect livery Freddie had ever seen whisked their luggage into the lobby.

Mrs. Bobbsey had just registered and turned toward the elevators, when who should come into the front door of the hotel but Daddy Bobbsey himself. Then there was a happy family reunion.

"Whee-ee," cried Freddie and Flossie together, grabbing their father around the neck.

Bert and Nan tried to act a little dignified but

were just as glad to see Daddy Bobbsey as the younger twins were.

"It's wonderful to be here," said Nan, her eyes shining.

"It's great," added Bert with a grin.

As soon as the greetings were over, Freddie announced that he was hungry. "We had breakfast very, very early," he said.

"As soon as you have washed and changed your clothes we shall have luncheon," promised Daddy Bobbsey. "Then you can tell me everything."

Staying at the big city hotel was a glorious adventure to the twins, especially to Freddie and Flossie. They admired the attractive elevator and the brown and gold suit of the boy who ran it. They liked the carpets which were so deep and soft that their feet sank into them.

"I guess it's just as well we didn't bring Waggo here," Flossie whispered as they followed the rigid back of the colored lad who was carrying their bags. "I'm sure they wouldn't like to have a dog in this place."

"No," said Freddie reluctantly. "I don't s'pose they would."

After the children had admired the comfortable rooms with baths which Mr. Bobbsey had engaged for them, the family went down to the hotel dining room for luncheon. The meal was almost like a feast; in fact, it *was* a feast, Daddy Bobbsey said, in celebration of the reunion with his family. While they ate they talked, for the twins were eager to tell of their trip and all the interesting things that had happened to them before leaving Lakeport.

In the course of the conversation the subject of the diamond ring came up. Mr. Bobbsey listened sympathetically while Nan told of the mysterious disappearance of the piece of jewelry as well as her desire to meet Miss Lila Lee and explain the matter to her.

"I want to get it over with, Daddy," she said unhappily. "The sooner the better!"

"All right, I'll arrange for you to see her. But please don't be upset, my dear," said Mr. Bobbsey, patting his daughter's arm. "I want you to enjoy your visit here. Now tell me what you would especially like to do in New York."

"May I tell what I want to do, too?" asked Freddie.

His father laughed. "Yes. In fact, I'd like to hear from each one of you. Nan first."

The girl smiled. "I'll tell you," she said, "if Bert won't laugh at me!"

CHAPTER XIII

AN INTERRUPTED LUNCHEON

ORDINARILY Bert Bobbsey liked to tease his twin, but he felt that this was no time to do so. His sister really needed cheering up, for she was worrying about the loss of the ring.

"I won't say a word," he promised, "not even if you want to go hear one of those sappy orchestra singers."

Nan laughed. "You certainly don't like them, do you?" she remarked. "Well, I don't either, unless they're good."

"They're never good," growled Bert.

"Wouldn't it be funny," giggled Flossie, "if you should turn out to be one some day, Bert?"

The Bobbseys laughed so merrily that the lad's face became very red. Finally he stammered, "I—I'm going to be a builder or somebody who works outdoors." Then he decided it was time to change the subject. "Let's—let's hear what Nan wants to do in New York," he said.

"Daddy," asked the older girl, "would I be allowed to visit a studio where people take lessons in stage dancing? I'd like to learn how it's done."

"I guess I can fix it up," said her father. "As soon as—oh Freddie!" he exclaimed.

A second before this a waiter had been about to put a plate of vanilla ice cream in front of Freddie, who was looking out of a window. The little boy had turned around quickly and bumped into the man's arm.

Bang! had gone the dish on the floor. Splash! had gone the milky dessert.

"Oh! Oh!" cried Freddie. "I'm awful sorry."

Mother and Daddy were embarrassed about the accident, but the waiter was very kind and said he had a small boy of his own who sometimes spilled things by mistake, too.

"I'll clean this up," he said, "and then I'll get you some more ice cream, little man."

"I—I guess I don't deserve any," quavered Freddie.

"That's all right," said the waiter.

He signalled to a boy in a white linen uniform. The lad came to the Bobbsey table with a funny looking contraption which he held by a handle. He snapped open a little lid, ran the machine along the floor, and in three seconds all the ice cream on the floor had disappeared inside the box.

"We ought to have one of those at our house,"

giggled Flossie. " 'Count of Freddie," she added.

Directly after luncheon Mr. Bobbsey phoned the broadcasting studio and was told that Miss Lila Lee had been called out of town for a few days. If Mr. Bobbsey would leave his name and address the company would be glad to give them to her upon her return. He thanked the voice at the other end of the wire, and then went to tell Nan of the conversation.

"I'm afraid your confession regarding the ring will have to be postponed a few days," he said. "While we are waiting for Miss Lila Lee to get back we will not be idle, though."

"What are we going to do, Daddy?" Freddie asked eagerly.

"My boy," said Mr. Bobbsey, "we are going to see the sights."

During the next few days Mr. Bobbsey kept his word to his family. First they rode up an elevator to the very top of the tallest building in the whole world. They looked over the railing of the high parapet on which they stood and saw people far below them who looked like crawling ants, while motor cars seemed like tiny shining beetles.

"I shouldn't like to fall over," said Flossie. "It makes me feel funny."

Daddy Bobbsey's arm tightened about her and he said. "I shouldn't like you to, little Fat Fairy."

Next they went to an aquarium to see a monster whale. Later, when they looked in the windows of a department store, Flossie saw a collection of dolls that enchanted her. There was a Dutch doll, a Japanese doll, and another one dressed in the costume of a Hungarian peasant.

"I believe this is the store that has the Dolls of All Nations exhibit," said Mrs. Bobbsey, recalling an advertisement in the morning paper. "Would you like to see it, Flossie? How about you, Nan?"

This program, of course, held little interest for the boys, a fact which they were quick to point out. It was finally agreed that Mrs. Bobbsey would go ahead with the girls. Mr. Bobbsey would take the boys to whatever place of entertainment they might choose for the afternoon.

"I want to see the biggest fire engine in the whole world," was Freddie's demand.

"Dad, could we first go to that famous hardware store you were telling us about, where they have all the wonderful tools?" Bert asked eagerly.

"A good choice, Son. Freddie will like that place too, I'm sure."

He and the boys said good-bye to the others and got on a bus. As Freddie thought it would be fun to ride on the top, they climbed the stairs.

No sooner had they sat down than the little fellow's hat blew off, so the three of them had to get off and chase the cap.

When they finally reached the big hardware store with its fascinating array of tools and electrical machines, the boys gazed in wonder at the things that met their eyes. There were tools of all sorts; little ones and big ones. What interested Bert most of all was an electric saw, a marvelous device that could cut through wood in a jiffy. A salesman who had been showing the Bobbsey party around asked the lad if he would like to see the machine in operation.

"Would I!" cried Bert. "I can't think of anything I'd like better, unless—"

"Unless what?" prompted the man encouragingly.

"Unless I could handle it all by myself," Bert finished eagerly. "I don't suppose I could, but I'd like to."

"Well, why not?" said the good-natured clerk. "I'll give you an idea of how it works, and then you can try it out for yourself. Now, look here."

With these words he picked up a large square of wood on which a picture had been drawn with black lines.

"The idea is to cut through the picture, using the lines as a guide. Then it can be hung up like a sign. Now I'll start the work and you can finish it."

Bert watched eagerly as the keen teeth bored neatly through the solid wood.

"You see, no pressure is needed at all," the salesman explained. "The idea is merely to guide the work. Electricity does the rest."

Bert was delighted to find that, after a short demonstration, he was able to operate the saw himself.

"With a little practice you could become an expert at the work," said the man.

After that Mr. Bobbsey had to buy Bert one of the marvelous tools. His son even thought he might go into the sign-making business!

"And how would you like to be a carpenter too, Freddie?" asked his father.

"I still want to be a fireman," the little fellow answered, "but maybe I could help Bert."

Freddie could not be overlooked for a present. After considerable deep thought on his part he finally chose a chest of drawers containing an assortment of tools of all kinds and sizes. The outside of the box was painted a bright red and had a picture of a firehouse on it.

"This may be a gentle hint to us," laughed Mr. Bobbsey, "that we haven't yet visited the firehouse."

"Oh yes, Daddy, let's go," urged Freddie, for he still had his mind set on seeing the biggest engine in the world.

At the nearest firehouse Mr. Bobbsey spoke to the pleasant fire chief, who smiled and said he didn't know whether they had the biggest fire engine in the world, but the one they had was pretty good at that.

"Come on, Son," he added, holding out a hand to Freddie, "I'll show you about the place and you can judge for yourself."

The half hour that followed was one of complete happiness for Freddie, who walked beside the fireman and took in every word he said. Their new friend even let him and Bert climb up on the engine while he explained various gadgets and tricks of fire-fighting to them.

Into the midst of all the fun there came a sudden clanging noise. The fire bell set up an urgent clamor, and instantly the place was full of shouts from firemen, who ran from different places, put on coats and helmets, and started the motors of the machines.

Freddie was thrilled, as the engine and hook-and-ladder trucks were manned by fire-fighters. A siren screeched, motors roared, and in a few moments the heavy trucks dashed out into the traffic-laden street.

Suddenly Mr. Bobbsey gripped Bert's arm. "Where's Freddie?" he shouted.

Bert started to say he did not know, then stopped suddenly as he caught a glimpse of his little brother.

"There!" he cried. "Oh Dad!"

Freddie had bobbed up between two ladders on the second truck! While his father and brother stared at him, and the machine moved swiftly down the street, the little boy smilingly waved his hand at the astonished pair.

CHAPTER XIV

A WILD ADVENTURE

THE noise and clangor of the fire engines died away. The piercing shriek of the siren grew fainter and finally was swallowed up in a tide of city sounds. Mr. Bobbsey and Bert stood at the entrance to the firehouse and stared after the hook-and-ladder truck as if they surely had been stunned.

"Freddie always wanted to go to a real fire on a fire truck and now I guess he has done it," said Bert.

"Yes, he has," cried Mr. Bobbsey. "But I'm afraid the men don't know it."

"And he may fall off!" Bert quavered.

"We'll have to go after him at once," said Daddy Bobbsey. "We'll try to find a taxi."

Meanwhile, Freddie was having the most thrilling time of his life. The hook-and-ladder truck tore through the crowded streets in the wake of the engine whose siren shrieked and shrieked. The little boy, clinging to the apparatus, felt like a king.

He knew that he had not been noticed thus far by the men, and he hoped that nobody would see him before they should reach the fire. Freddie did not want to be stopped, now that he was about to realize his dearest ambition—to go to a real fire with real firemen on a real up-to-date hook-and-ladder truck.

He could see how people scuttled out of the path of the engine, and how traffic in the street opened to make way for it. He almost laughed out loud as the truck swung around the corner, skidded crazily, and then came to a stop close to an apartment building from which smoke and flames were coming.

Perhaps Freddie did laugh out loud; at any rate, he suddenly felt a strong hand laid on his shoulder and heard a surprised voice say, "Well, of all things. Where did this kid come from?"

The little boy looked up to find himself staring into the bronzed face and angry blue eyes of one of the firemen, who gave Freddie a little shake.

"Where did you come from?" he demanded. "How did you get on this hook-and-ladder? You young scamp. You ought to be arrested."

With this he handed the little Bobbsey lad over

to a second fireman. Confused and a trifle frightened, Freddie found himself being hustled back until he reached several policemen who were trying to keep a crowd of people away from the burning building. One of them asked where his parents were.

"I don't know," replied the little boy, his lower lip beginning to tremble. "I left my daddy back at the firehouse. I guess prob'bly most likely he's still there."

"Well, you stay with me, Son," said the policeman quickly. "You had no business to come here. But maybe your dad will show up. If he doesn't, you'll have to come with me to the station house. A crowd like this is no place for a little fellow like you. You'll get hurt."

Freddie was beginning to agree with him. The throngs were getting denser every minute. People jostled one another about and pushed this way and that way in an effort to get a closer view of the fire. People stepped on Freddie, knocked off his cap, and otherwise mishandled him. Things might have gone very hard with the little boy had it not been for the policeman.

Even so, Freddie was beginning to feel a little worried when there was a disturbance in the crowd close to him, and he heard his daddy's voice saying, almost in his ear:

"Here he is, the young rascal! I told you we'd find him in the thick of things."

The little boy flung himself upon Mr. Bobbsey and clung closely to him.

"I'm so glad you've come!" he cried. "It was fun at first, but then they took me off the truck and the policeman said maybe he'd have to arrest me. Golly! I wouldn't like that. Not much!"

The police officer met Mr. Bobbsey's look, and he smiled and touched his cap.

"I was all for taking him to Headquarters, sir, until you turned up," he explained.

Mr. Bobbsey took a firm grip of Freddie's hand. "Thanks for taking care of him, Officer. I'm much obliged to you."

"Not at all, sir," said the man. "And young fellow," he added, "don't run away from your father again."

Meanwhile, what of Nan and Flossie? While Bert had been trying the electric saw and Freddie was, as usual, getting himself into trouble, the girls and Mrs. Bobbsey were enjoying adventures of their own which were, in their way, every bit as exciting as those of Freddie and Bert.

As soon as the boys and Mr. Bobbsey were out of sight Mrs. Bobbsey had led Nan and Flossie into the store which had advertised the Dolls of All Nations exhibit.

They took an elevator to the third floor, where a clerk directed them to the proper department. There, arranged cleverly on two long counters, were the dolls—rows upon rows of them, each one dressed in costume. The features and headgear of each one bore the stamp of the country it represented.

"How *real* the dolls look!" cried Flossie. "Mother, may I have one? I like the little Chinese girl best."

A smiling clerk explained that the one Flossie liked was really and truly Chinese, for everything about it had been made in China. Mrs. Bobbsey bought the doll, to the great delight of her little daughter, who refused to have her treasure wrapped in a box, and insisted upon carrying it about with her.

"I want to look at her a lot," Flossie said.

Asked what she would like, Nan Bobbsey chose a Spanish masquerade costume. It was a charming outfit, complete from its red blouse and flaring skirt to the high jewelled comb and lace mantilla.

Nan tried on the costume to make sure it was her size. When she walked out of the fitting room a few minutes later no native girl could have looked more Spanish than Nan did—or so Flossie thought.

"It suits you, dear, and it fits perfectly," Mrs.

Bobbsey said approvingly. "Turn around so that I can see the back."

As Nan did so, the saleswoman was struck by an interesting thought.

"Why don't you wear your costume to the Dances of All Nations exhibit?" she suggested. "It is to be given in the store auditorium in about half an hour and I understand a great many of the children in the audience will come in costume."

Both Flossie and Mrs. Bobbsey thought this was a very good idea. Though Nan hesitated a little at first, she finally was persuaded by her mother and sister to go to the exhibit in her new Spanish outfit.

The Bobbseys went down to the auditorium at once since Nan did not want to walk around the store in costume. They found they had a while to wait before the performance should begin, so they spent the time pleasantly in watching the people who came in, and in commenting upon the various masquerades worn by the children in the audience.

"I like yours best, Nan," whispered Flossie loyally.

At last, when they were beginning to get a little tired of waiting, the orchestra struck up a lively Scotch air. Soon the stage was filled with pretty girls in kilt and tartan dancing the Highland Fling. This number won hearty applause from the audience. It was followed by folk dances of several other countries.

There was a rather long pause in the program after the last of these. As the audience began to grow impatient, the manager appeared on the stage. The buzz of conversation died down when he lifted his hand for attention.

"I regret to have to announce," he said, "that the next number on our program will have to be omitted. Our Spanish dancer has been taken ill suddenly and will not be able to go on with her performance."

At this point Flossie jumped to her feet.

"My sister can do the dance for you," she cried eagerly. "She really is a very good dancer, and she even has on a Spanish costume."

Poor Nan was crimson with embarrassment.

"Do hush, Flossie!" she cried, and pulled her little sister down beside her.

It was too late, however. The eyes of the manager were upon Nan in her pretty Spanish dress. He leaned toward her from the stage and spoke to her.

"I wish the young lady would come up on the platform," he said. "There is nothing to be afraid of. And I am sure the audience as well as myself will be very grateful if you will dance for them in place of our little senorita, who unfortunately is ill."

Urged by her mother and Flossie, with the applause of the audience to spur her on, Nan rose slowly and made her way to the stage. As she walked up the steps the manager took her by the hand and led her to the center of the platform.

As she looked down at the countless upraised faces in the audience, Nan was seized by a strange feeling. Her knees felt weak and her hands were like ice. Then the orchestra struck up a gay Spanish tune. As the girl hesitated, the leader nodded encouragingly and raised his baton.

Nan obeyed the signal as if she were in a daze, and began to dance; at first awkwardly, then more easily as her feet caught the rhythm of the music. Gradually she forgot that strangers were watching her. The tune caught her up and whirled her about. She felt as though she were floating on air.

After that it was sheer fun. Nan finished dancing in a whirl of skirts and flying mantilla. She made a deep curtsey in response to a burst of applause from the audience. A moment later, excited and happy, she slipped into her seat beside Flossie.

"Was I all right?" she asked breathlessly.

"You were awfully good, Nan," said Flossie, hugging her sister. "I guess you will win first prize."

"I don't believe there are any prizes," Nan answered.

But there were; and when the awards were announced it was found that first prize went to the group of Scotch lassies, the second to Anna Loy, Japanese dancer, and the third one to—Miss Nan Bobbsey!

CHAPTER XV

A FUNNY MISTAKE

WHAT a wonderful day it had been for them all!
And what tales the Bobbseys had to tell one another when they met that night at dinnertime!

Bert brought out his wonderful new saw, while
Freddie displayed his bright red chest of tools.
Nan then told of her experience at the Dances of
All Nations exhibit, and Flossie placed her Chi-
nese doll in the most prominent position in the
room so that all might admire it.

"I have something to show you, too," Mr. Bobbsey announced as he took an envelope from his
pocket. "The clerk at the desk handed it to me.
I've looked inside and find it contains tickets ad-
mitting us to a splendid show in radioland; one
in which Miss Lila Lee sings."

Nan quickly looked up and her face clouded.
"Is Miss Lee back then, Daddy?" she asked.

"Not yet, but I believe the studio expects her
to return in a day or two. At that time," added
Mr. Bobbsey with an understanding glance at his

daughter, "we must pay the lady the compliment of a visit."

"I suppose so," said his daughter, "but I hate to have to tell her about the diamond ring."

Poor Nan! The loss of the jewelry preyed on her mind so that she could hardly shake it off. She thought about it the first thing each morning and the last thing every night. Even the pleasure of this delightful visit to the city was dimmed by it.

"If I could only find the ring, everything would be all right again," she thought wistfully. "But there's no use in hoping that. I might just as well wish for the moon."

The girl's dark mood lasted for the rest of the evening, even troubling her dreams during the night. Morning, however, brought her brighter thoughts, and the loss of the diamond took its proper place once more in the scheme of things.

First of all, Mr. Ken Speer phoned to ask the Bobbsey family to visit him at his studio the following day. This pleased the twins greatly, for they had taken a fancy to the pleasant playwright and were eager to see him again.

"Maybe he will write us another play," Flossie stated.

"You must not suggest any such thing, my dear," said Mrs. Bobbsey, alarmed at the idea. "Mr. Speer is a very busy man. It's kind of him to invite us all to his studio, but we must be very careful not to impose upon him."

"Suppose we practice our play today," Nan suggested. "We haven't had a rehearsal since we left home; and Daddy's birthday will be here before we know it."

"Golly, I bet Flossie has forgotten all about how to cry in the first scene," said Freddie, who was piling books and magazines on the floor to make a railroad tunnel.

"I have not," his twin returned indignantly. "I guess I can cry now just as well as I ever did!"

"We'll soon see about that," said Nan. She began moving the furniture about in preparation for the first scene. "If we hope to have the play ready in time I think we need a good long rehearsal," she added.

The children agreed with their sister, and bustled about the hotel bedrooms helping her set the stage. When everything was ready Freddie said suddenly:

"I don't see how we can act our play without Waggo. We must have him bark and dig up the diamond ring."

"Bert can take Waggo's part," Nan said quickly. "He has to most of the time, anyway, because Waggo can never remember to bark at the right time. Now, then, is everybody ready?"

"Wait a minute," said Flossie. "I've got to get my foot out. It's stuck under a cushion."

"Well, get it out and be quick about it," urged stage manager Nan. "It's time for Act I to begin."

"All right," said Flossie. "It's out. And now I begin to cry."

"Quiet, everybody!" ordered Nan. "Spotlight! Curtain! All right, Flossie. Begin!"

Flossie covered her face with her chubby hands and whimpered pitifully. The play was on!

After half an hour or so of acting on the part of the Bobbsey twins things began to happen in the hall outside their rooms. A colored boy in hotel livery passing through the corridor heard the bark of a dog and paused to listen.

"Ain't no dogs allowed here," he thought, and pressed close to the Bobbsey door.

What he heard made him much more surprised. The conversation was a strange one, all about diamond rings and missing aunts. Once the hall boy was sure he heard a little girl crying as if her heart would break.

"Something mighty funny going on in there," thought the lad. "Needs looking into, all right."

Another bellhop chanced to pass by at that moment, and the boy beckoned to him.

"Listen, and see what you think of the

goings-on in there," the lad whispered. "Sounds pretty queer to me."

The second fellow listened intently, a look of deepest surprise on his face. Then he heard Nan say in tragic tones:

"All these years I have longed to see you. No one knows how I have looked forward to this meeting. And now that it has come, what do I find? That you have taken my beautiful ring!"

The two lads outside the door exchanged glances. One of them raised his eyebrows questioningly; the other nodded seriously.

"Jewel thieves!" said he.

"Listen!" the other commanded.

On the opposite side of the door there came sounds of bitterest sobbing, which in another moment were interrupted by the excited barking of a dog.

"Dogs ain't allowed here," muttered one of the boys, scowling.

"Must have been smuggled in," the other nodded.

Meanwhile the crying within the room had stopped.

"Waggo, darling Waggo," cried Nan after a brief pause, "you have dug up the diamond ring!"

The astonished hall boys waited to hear no more. It was plain to them now that something very queer was going on behind the closed door of Room 332, and they meant to find out what it was without further delay.

They located the hotel detective in the manager's room, and poured forth their story into his ears. When they had finished he nodded thoughtfully and rose to his feet.

"May be thieves and smugglers, or else those folks are just plain crazy," he commented. "Anyway, we'll soon find out, and put them where they belong."

When the detective and the two hall boys reached Room 332 the twins had begun rehearsing the last act all over again. Thus it happened that the detective heard the same thing that the two lads had heard previously—the running down of Nan by the rich aunt, the heartbroken sobbing of the little girl, Waggo's excited barks, and finally the finding of the diamond ring.

The detective straightened his shoulders and nodded meaningly.

"Sounds like jewel thieves, all right," he said. "I guess it's about time for me to do something."

He knocked sharply on the door.

CHAPTER XVI

THE RADIO CHILD

INSTANTLY there was silence within the room where the Bobbsey twins were acting. This was followed by an excited scrabbling and the sound of furniture being pushed about.

The detective knocked again, this time more sharply. It was the kind of knock which usually brings an immediate response, and it did this time. The door opened and a pretty woman, her hair slightly untidy, stood in the doorway.

"Yes?" said Mrs. Bobbsey. "What is it you want?"

The detective pushed past her, followed more respectfully by the two hall boys.

"I want to know what's going on here," said the officer, looking about him with small, bright eyes that took in everything at a glance. "What's all this about a diamond ring? And I heard a dog bark, too. Don't you know that dogs are not allowed in this hotel?"

The twins had clustered about their mother.

Bert, angered by the detective's tone, was regarding him with flashing eyes.

"Diamond ring? Dogs?" Mrs. Bobbsey spoke, puzzled.

Suddenly Nan began to laugh. "Don't you see?" she explained. "This man must have heard Bert barking and thought it was a real dog. And the diamond ring—"

"Yes, what about the diamond ring?" the detective demanded gruffly. "Say, what kind of a show is this, anyway?"

"That's just it—it *is* a show. My children were rehearsing a play," Mrs. Bobbsey explained. Then she added with a smile, "There isn't any mystery, really. If you will just sit down a moment I will explain everything to you."

The detective looked at the gaping hall boys, told them to run along, and then sat down on the edge of a chair. His manner seemed to say that he would stand no nonsense and that the explanation had better be a good one or Mrs. Bobbsey need not expect him to believe it.

However, instead of telling the man anything, Mrs. Bobbsey did the best thing she could possibly have done. She made the children go over the last scene again exactly as they had done it while the detective had waited outside the door. At the end the audience of one was laughing. Not only was he convinced, but was genuinely enthusiastic over the children's performance.

"They're mighty good," he said. "And that little girl over there," pointing to Flossie, "looks and speaks exactly like Flossie Fair, the child radio star."

Of course, it was very interesting to the Bobbseys to hear that Flossie looked so much like another little fair-haired girl who was already famous over the radio and who, as rumor had it, was soon to sign a motion picture contract as well.

Flossie Bobbsey was thrilled. "Does she really look an awful lot like me?" she asked, leaning against the detective's knee and gazing up into his face. "Has she yellow hair and blue eyes and is she fat, too? Daddy calls me his little fat fairy, you know."

The detective laughed and patted Flossie's hand.

"I should say Flossie Fair was just about your size, little miss," he said. "I know her, too, and also her folks. Maybe you'd like to meet her some time."

"Oh, I would, wouldn't I, Mother?" said Flossie, turning to Mrs. Bobbsey eagerly. "We should all like to meet her very much, Mr. Detective."

"Curry's the name," said the sleuth, getting to his feet, "and I'll see what I can do about arranging a meeting with Flossie Fair. The little girl's on her way home from Europe now, but the boat's due to dock pretty soon and then we'll see what can be done."

He paused to stare at Flossie and scratched his head thoughtfully.

"I never did see a stronger resemblance," he said. "It's really astonishing, so it is. If you were to exchange one for the other I'm sure no one would know the difference."

After the detective had gone the Bobbseys discussed his visit for a long time, especially that part of it which had to do with the reported resemblance between their own Flossie and little Flossie Fair, the radio star.

When they told Daddy Bobbsey about it that night he said that he was sure his Flossie was much nicer than Flossie Fair, even though the two little girls did look alike, and that he would never exchange his fat fairy for any one else, no matter what might happen.

The next day the Bobbsey family went over to visit Ken Speer. Daddy Bobbsey, however, could not go as he had to attend to his business.

The playwright had a funny, narrow little house which was squeezed in so tightly between two larger ones that it gave the impression of being held up by them. Freddie was quite sure that if either of the larger houses were to be taken away suddenly the playwright's tiny one would crumple right down on the sidewalk like a deck of cards.

Inside it was even odder than outside, and was so full of queer little steps and odd passages that the children were fascinated by it. The whole top floor had been given over to studios. In the art room Ken Speer showed them a little theatre which he had had built for him and which was an exact model of an actual stage.

"Look, it even has little footlights," Nan cried delightedly. "Do they really light up, Mr. Speer?"

"Of course," smiled the playwright. "Come here, Bert," he said. "Touch that switch and see what happens."

The twins cried out with delight as the make-believe stage was flooded with radiance.

"This is the workshop where I try out most of my settings before they come to the stage," Mr. Speer told them. "Now I want you to have lunch with me," he added, "and after that I will show you my printing press."

"Printing press," Bert repeated. "Do you print your plays too, Mr. Speer?"

"No," laughed the playwright. "My press is more of a hobby than anything else. But it works I'll show you after luncheon."

The twins were too excited to do much justice to Mr. Speer's excellent meal. As soon as it was over and they could do so without being rude, they urged their kind friend to take them to see the printing press.

The children were so fascinated by this new toy that Mr. Speer offered to show them how a real book could be made in his own workshop.

"Golly! Can you make a book?" cried Freddie, staring at the playwright as if he were a new sort of magician.

"Why, of course," smiled Ken Speer. "And the nice thing about it is that you can help me if you like. Come, I'll show you what to do."

Under the expert guidance of their good friend the twins set to work to make a little book all their own.

Bert composed and typed an original fairy tale about two hundred words in length. While he was doing this Nan set to work to draw the pictures for it. They were not works of art, but then, as she said herself, in a fairy story anything can be possible. If the tail of her fire-eating monster was short and stubby and its neck resembled that of a giraffe, who was to say that all fire-eating monsters did not have giraffes' necks and short, stubby tails? Certainly not the twins!

Before Nan had finished her drawings the children were in such gales of laughter that it was almost impossible for them to go on with their work.

They persisted in their efforts, however, and at last the great work, including a cover design by Flossie, was ready for the press. Freddie, who had helped set the machine, now assisted the playwright to operate it while the other children looked on eagerly.

Then, without warning, there came a sudden painful cry from the small twin.

"Ouch! Ouch! Stop the machine!"

Instantly work ceased. The presses became silent, but Freddie continued to cry.

Bert sprang to his brother's side. "Did you get pinched? Are you hurt?"

Flossie began to kiss her twin. "Oh, don't cry, Freddie. Please don't cry," she begged tenderly.

Nan held the little lad's fingers in her own. One thumb was turning a bit purple on the end. Mr. Speer, seeing the trouble, drew a cup of cold water from a nearby cooler. Freddie dipped his finger into the paper container.

"Oh, that feels good," he sighed. "I'm better now, Mr. Speer. Let's finish the book."

The playwright laughed. "You're a brave scout, Freddie. Your motto is 'Nothing must interfere with progress,' I guess."

At last the work was done—the book of the Bobbsey twins themselves.

"It's lovely," agreed Mrs. Bobbsey when they gave it to her to inspect. "I never dreamed I had such an artistic family."

"I guess I'll be a printer when I grow up," Freddie announced importantly. "It's loads of fun."

All in all, the children could not remember when they had ever had a happier day. They said good-bye to Mr. Ken Speer and promised to come to see him again as soon as they possibly could.

It was perhaps natural that after such an exciting day the children should find it a little hard to get to sleep that night. They certainly did lie awake much longer than usual. When they dozed off at last their rest was uneasy.

Nan dreamed that she was wandering down a strange street with no beginning and no end. Suddenly she turned a corner and found herself facing a high brick wall. While she stood watching the wall it began to topple toward her.

She jumped to one side, and as she did so the partition fell with a dreadful crash! She cried out in fear, and wakened to find herself sitting straight up in bed, the noise of the crash still in her ears.

She heard it a second time, and realized that what had awakened her was really thunder. A terrific storm was raging. The rain beat against the windows, and the sky was torn again and again by flashes of yellow lightning.

Nan jumped out of bed and pushed the electric light switch, but nothing happened. The room stayed in darkness, save when the lightning flashed. Then she heard her father's voice outside in the hall calling Bert's name anxiously. She ran to the door and flung it open.

CHAPTER XVII

NO LIGHTS

THE thunder and lightning roused Bert Bobbsey several minutes before it did his father. He heard a strange cry, too. Rubbing his sleepy eyes, he jumped up.

"Oh! Oh! I can't see—I can't see!" wailed a voice in the hallway.

Bert pulled on a robe and slippers. Then he stepped into the hotel corridor. It was pitch black. What was the reason? Perhaps the engineers at the city power plant had turned off the electric current for the sake of safety, he thought.

Again the worried voice called, "Somebody come and help me! Oh, please take pity on me!"

"Where are you?" cried Bert cheerily. "I'll come to you as soon as I can locate you."

"Here, here," said the voice, "down near the elevator!"

Bert Bobbsey hurried as best he could in the inky blackness toward the sound. Presently the cry came closer and then a cold, bony hand clutched the lad's ankle.

It was so spooky and strange that Bert felt a shiver run down his spine. Who was holding his limb so tightly? He would rather it had been a tackle on a football field than in a strange hotel hallway as black as an ancient dungeon.

"Oh!" said the trembling voice, "now I'm better. I can lift myself. Are you strong?"

"Yes," gasped the Bobbsey boy, "I'm—I'm very strong. *What is the matter?*"

"I've lost my crutch. I can't stand up."

Then Bert knew that the speaker must be an old soldier he had seen in the hotel and that the man really needed help to right himself.

"I'll look for it, sir, at once. Don't worry."

"Fine, my lad. You've a good head on you. You'll make a great general."

Bert crawled on his hands and knees over the thick carpet, feeling his way slowly. Suddenly his hand came in contact with the wooden prop.

"I have it. Here, take it as I lift you up."

Painfully and slowly the one-legged soldier drew himself up.

"Thanks a thousand times, Son."

A heavy peal of thunder cut into the sentence. It made the veteran think of war, and he trembled nervously.

"It's all right," said Bert. "Glad I could do it. Now, where is your room? I'll help you to it."

"Across from the elevator."

Bert fumbled at the door and opened it with the man's key. As he helped the cripple into the room, he felt the veteran was secure at last. However, the soldier did not want the lad to leave.

"You must come inside," he insisted, and banged the door shut.

Meanwhile Nan Bobbsey had been awakened in her bedroom by the sound of voices in the hallway. As she stepped to the door she heard someone say:

"The electric wires must be down. There isn't a light in the place."

"Bert, Bert, where are you?" Mr. Bobbsey was calling.

Nan caught her father's arm as he brushed past her.

"Daddy, what's the matter?" she cried. "Has anything happened to Bert?"

Mr. Bobbsey bent toward his daughter, trying to see through the darkness. "Oh, it's you, Nan."

"Daddy, where is Bert?" the girl persisted, growing frightened. "Has anything happened to him?"

A crash of thunder cut off the last part of her sentence. When the deep rumblings ceased she pointed to a faint beam far down the corridor.

"Maybe that's Bert's flashlight," she said.

Other people who had been aroused by the storm, were alarmed at the failure of the lights to turn on, and had come out into the hall to see what was wrong. Mr. Bobbsey inquired of them as to Bert's whereabouts. No one recalled having seen a boy with a flashlight running down the hall.

"Where do you suppose Bert could have gone?" Nan demanded anxiously.

Meanwhile emergency lights had been put on in the hotel and sleepy attendants were going from door to door telling the guests not to worry, and promising quick repair work on the damaged electric wires.

Mr. Bobbsey and Nan had just about decided to go back to their rooms in the hope that Bert might have returned by a different route, when they came face to face with the lad himself.

"Hello," he grinned. "Were you looking for something?"

"We were looking for you," said Nan, "and getting worried. Where have you been?"

As they went back to their rooms Bert explained about finding the cripple.

"I hope you got the old soldier back to his room all right," said Mr. Bobbsey.

"Oh yes," laughed Bert. "I found his crutch and he had his key, so it was only a matter of a little time before we got to the right room. He wanted me to stay, but I told him I shouldn't."

When Mr. Bobbsey, Bert and Nan reached their quarters they found Mrs. Bobbsey and the little twins awake and anxiously awaiting them. They told what had happened. Then the whole family scattered to their rooms to make up, as best they could, their hour of broken sleep.

They awakened next morning to a dreary, drizzling day. Rain continued to fall for hours and hours. By late afternoon the Bobbsey twins were so restless that they were ready to do almost anything for a change. When Mr. Bobbsey, returned he suggested that they all go by an underground route to visit the radio studio for which he had been given tickets, the children seized upon the suggestion eagerly.

"Ho! Ho!" roared Freddie.

Flossie clapped her hands, as Nan and Bert together said, "That'll be great!"

The twins were very much interested to find that it was not necessary for them to go into the street at all to reach the studio. They merely walked down to the basement of the hotel where there was an entrance into the subway. From that place they continued on through a brilliantly lighted arcade which was lined with shops. In these shops almost anything could be bought, clothing, drugs, even strawberry jam!

"But why do men and women have stores underground, Daddy?" asked Flossie, her eyes round with wonder. "Isn't there enough room on top of the ground? And do people really buy things in these stores?"

"I should say so, Fat Fairy," laughed Mr. Bobbsey. "You see, they can stop in and buy various things on their way to a subway train."

"It's like a city under a city," said Bert in an awed voice. "I guess you could pretty nearly live underground if you wanted to, couldn't you, Dad?"

"Very nearly," agreed Mr. Bobbsey. "Most of the big office buildings and stores are connected with the subways. A great many of the hotels are too, and even some of the theatres. So you could live, travel, buy food and clothes, go to business and even to the theatre, if you cared to, without setting foot above ground."

This was a very strange and interesting idea to the twins. They thought about it while they entered another brightly-lighted building and were whirled up in an elevator to the eighteenth floor. Here were the offices of the broadcasting company. After they had been greeted courteously, the Bobbseys were led into a balcony room. There they were permitted to look down through a large plate glass window into a studio.

"You are in luck," the attendant told them. "Miss Lila Lee has just returned from an important trip. Her program will be next. Ah!" he added, as a tall, beautifully-dressed woman entered the studio and approached the microphone, "there she is now! Believe me, you have a treat in store for you."

Mrs. Bobbsey stole a look at Nan and saw how the mention of Lila Lee's name had clouded her daughter's face. The girl met her mother's glance and nodded miserably.

"I'll tell her about the ring right after the broadcast," she whispered. "I'll be glad to get it over. Oh, Mother—"

The attendant hissed, "Silence, please!" and Nan stopped talking.

Miss Lee had a beautiful voice and sang songs pleasing to people of all ages. The program included selections by an orchestra also, and all the Bobbseys enjoyed it immensely—except Nan. The worried girl could think of nothing but the confession she must make as soon as the broadcast should be over.

"Oh, I wish the ring had never been lost," she sighed.

When Miss Lee finally left the microphone and glided gracefully toward the exit at the rear of the studio, Nan slipped away unobserved by any of her family. She had made up her mind to speak to Miss Lee at the very earliest possible moment! Now that the time had come for her to do so she was eager to confess the loss of the diamond ring while she still had the courage to speak.

She was not sure which way to turn to find Miss Lee, but luck was with her. She saw the singer walking down a corridor and ran toward the young woman, who opened a door and went through. Nan reached the spot. Without giving herself time to think she rapped smartly on the door.

A musical voice said "Come in."

Nan slipped inside, closed the door quietly, and stood with her back against it.

"Miss Lee," she began, then stopped.

The singer looked at the girl in surprise. But the gray eyes which regarded Nan so curiously were very friendly.

"What is it, my dear?" asked Miss Lee. "Is there anything I can do for you? Your face is familiar. Have I met you before?"

The voice in which the questions were asked was so kind that Nan decided to tell the whole story of the diamond ring at once. This she did, telling first who she was, then going on, the words tumbling from her eager lips.

"I can't believe yet that the ring is lost for good," she concluded earnestly. "You see, I put it away so carefully in my handkerchief case that I feel sure it must still be in our house somewhere. I'll hunt for it again, I promise, as soon as we get back to Lakeport."

"Of course you will, and I am quite sure you'll find it," said Miss Lee kindly, after she got over her astonishment at learning who Nan was, and how the girl had found her. "Come here, my dear," she added, motioning her young caller to her side. "You have been worrying a great deal about this, haven't you?" she asked.

Nan's eyes filled with tears and her lips quivered. "I've been ashamed to tell you about it," she confessed. "It was so careless of me to lose the ring."

"But it was still more careless of *me* to lose it in the first place," the singer pointed out. "If any one is to blame, surely it is I. And now let's talk about something pleasant," she coaxed, smiling. "Tell me about my sister whom I want so much to see after all these years. Come, talk to me and let me see you smile again."

Drawn by the questions of the young woman, Nan found herself relating all about her Lakeport friends, and the glorious adventures of the past few days in the city. She had just finished the story of the rehearsal of their play in the hotel room, and Miss Lee had been laughing heartily over the queer mistake of the hotel detective, when the whole Bobbsey family appeared at the door of the room.

"Oh," said Nan, "I want you to meet all my family—my mother and father and the twins."

The singer nodded courteously. Then she looked at Flossie in amazement.

"My dear little girl," she said to the Bobbsey twin, rising to her feet dramatically. "The detective was right in what he said. You are the very image of Flossie Fair!"

CHAPTER XVIII

FUN IN THE STUDIO

FLOSSIE BOBBSEY, who had almost forgotten about looking like Flossie Fair, the little radio star, seemed rather startled at Miss Lee's exclamation. She made no protest, however, when the woman took her by the hand and drew her into the room. She merely looked back at Mother and Daddy Bobbsey and was glad to see that they were following her and were smiling as though at a good joke.

"I have heard before that our fat fairy looks very much like a certain young person of importance," smiled Mr. Bobbsey. "We are even beginning to believe that such is the case."

"The likeness to Flossie Fair is extraordinary," said Miss Lee, taking the little fat fairy over to the light. "I am amazed that I did not notice it the day I stopped at your house."

"It was dark in our hall," said Flossie.

"I'd like to show this child to the manager of the auditions department," said the star impulsively. "Would you have any objection?" she asked, turning to Mr. and Mrs. Bobbsey.

"On the contrary, I think it might be very interesting," said Mrs. Bobbsey. Daddy Bobbsey seemed inclined to object at first, but was finally overruled by Miss Lee's enthusiasm.

In the auditions department Flossie felt shy again, especially when a man with a sharp nose and keen gray eyes drew her up to him and scanned her face intently.

"Remarkable," he said, lifting his head with a quick, bird-like gesture. He shot a glance at the others in the group, but his eyes returned almost at once to Flossie. "Now let me hear you speak, my dear," he commanded. "Say something."

Flossie looked confused.

"I—I don't know what to say," stammered the little girl.

"That's enough," said the manager. To Flossie's surprise he smiled most agreeably at her parents and Miss Lee. "Even the voice is the same as Flossie Fair's," he said. "Let's try it over the air."

When a microphone was placed before Flossie and arranged so that she could talk into it the little girl was at first shy, but this feeling rapidly changed into one of excitement and keen interest.

"Can people really hear what I say?" she asked.

"They can in the studio," the sharp-faced man assured her. "Do you know a poem?" he asked abruptly.

"I know 'The Night Before Christmas,' " said Flossie.

"Right! Say it now and use your own voice. Talk right into the mike. That's it."

Flossie recited the poem from beginning to end. She made two mistakes, but they were only small ones and the little girl hoped no one noticed them.

In a few moments word came from the studio that the new child's voice was identical to that of Flossie Fair. No one in a radio audience could possibly notice any difference.

"What does 'dentical mean, Daddy?" Flossie asked.

"It means the same as," Daddy Bobbsey explained.

"Your little girl could double for Flossie Fair any time she cares to," the manager said. "Voice, looks, height and build—everything. I've never seen such a striking resemblance before. Does she sing?" he added in his pouncing way.

Mr. Bobbsey shook his head, but Flossie said

ambitiously, "Maybe I could if I learned how. I think it would be nice to know how to sing the way Miss Lee does."

The lady smiled and patted the little girl's cheek.

"Maybe you will, dear, some day," she said. "Who knows?"

It was about this time that Freddie, who had been examining the microphone with the greatest curiosity, demanded that his voice be tested, too.

Mr. and Mrs. Bobbsey said no, that they had already taken up too much of the busy manager's time. However, Miss Lee came to Freddie's aid.

"It will only take a few moments to try out his voice," she stated. "Perhaps," with a glance at the eager faces of the older children, "Nan and Bert would like to have their voices recorded, too."

Mr. and Mrs. Bobbsey made no objection. Amid a good deal of fun and laughter the amateur broadcast went forward. The twins entered into the spirit of the thing with such enthusiasm that even the manager lost his bored expression after a moment or two and became very much interested.

When the report came in from the studio that each of them had perfect broadcasting tones, Miss Lee clapped her hands with pleasure.

"The youngsters are good," said the manager thoughtfully. "I'd like to try them out in a little skit some time in something that they can all put on together."

"Maybe we could act out our play," said Freddie sturdily. "It's a good one even if the hotel 'tective did say we had a dog in our rooms."

The manager seemed so interested that in the end Freddie told him all about the play and the rehearsal they had had in their hotel room. The result was that the manager suggested they rehearse again right there in his office in front of the microphone.

It was the greatest fun in the world, even if the children were a little timid before the mike at first. Their stage-fright soon disappeared, however, and they went through the play from beginning to end, giving a much better performance than they had ever done before.

The manager seemed to like it very much, and praised the script highly.

"It's well done," he said. "Shows good workmanship."

"It should be good," said Bert loyally. "Mr. Speer wrote it for us."

The manager looked up sharply.

"Ken Speer, the famous playwright?" he queried.

"Yes, sir, he's a friend of ours," stated Bert proudly.

"Do you know him, Mr. Manager?" asked Flossie.

"Know Ken Speer?" he replied. "I guess I do. He happens to be a friend of *mine,* too. No wonder your playlet is good," he added warmly, "since Ken Speer had a hand in it."

Before the Bobbseys left his office the manager had taken their address, had shaken hands with them very cordially and invited them to call again some time.

"He likes you Bobbsey twins," Miss Lee whispered to them outside the manager's door. "He liked your skit, too. He might even use it some time."

"Over the air?" breathed Nan.

"Where else?" returned Miss Lee, smiling.

She waved to them gaily and hurried off toward her dressing room.

When Daddy Bobbsey said, "Come along, now, it's time we started for the hotel," Nan stood quite still in the hall outside the manager's room, staring after Lila Lee. It was not until her mother touched her on the shoulder that Nan turned and followed her family from the broadcasting station.

"Mother," she said some minutes later as they

were nearing their hotel, "do people get much money for broadcasting over the air?"

"Why yes, dear, they certainly do," Mrs. Bobbsey replied. "I understand radio performers are paid very well. Some, of course, are more popular than others and get far more for their services."

"Enough to—to buy diamond rings?" asked Nan breathlessly.

Mrs. Bobbsey regarded her daughter thoughtfully.

"Why yes, I suppose so. But just what are you getting at, Nan?"

Instead of answering, the girl drew her mother over to the window of a jewelry store.

"I'd like to look at something in here. Will you come with me?" she asked.

Mrs. Bobbsey assented, wondering. She became still more puzzled when Nan asked to see a tray of diamond rings.

CHAPTER XIX

"I LIKE this one," she said, pointing to a flawless white diamond in a lovely platinum setting. "Will you please tell me the price of it?"

The salesman picked up the ring and held it to the light.

"A beautiful diamond, Miss," he said. "This one costs five hundred dollars."

"Oh, thank you very much," said Nan in a faint voice.

She caught her mother's hand and hurried from the store.

"But Nan, dear, I don't understand," Mrs. Bobbsey protested. "Why did you ask the price of a beautiful diamond like that?"

"I know you will think me silly, Mother, and I don't blame you for laughing at me," said poor Nan, "but I did feel, just for a minute, that I might be able to buy the ring, not right now, of course, but some day. I—I didn't think it would cost so much."

154

"I'm not laughing at you, dear, and I think I understand," said Mrs. Bobbsey gently. "You are still worrying about Miss Lee's lost ring and you want to buy her one to take its place. Is that it?"

Nan nodded, not trusting herself to speak.

"But how do you expect to make so much money, Nan?" Mrs. Bobbsey went on gently.

"If I tell you, you *will* laugh," replied Nan desperately.

"Of course I won't. Now go ahead and tell me before we reach the hotel. You don't want the others to hear you, do you?"

"It's only that I thought—when Miss Lee said the audition manager might let us broadcast— that I could make some money that way. I wanted it to buy Miss Lee a new ring, that's all. I know it's foolish of me, Mother, but anyway," with a burst of thankfulness, *"you didn't laugh!"*

Mrs. Bobbsey was far from laughing as she looked at her daughter's troubled face and realized, perhaps for the first time, how deeply Nan had taken to heart the loss of the diamond ring. That night she spoke to Daddy Bobbsey about it.

"If you think it best," he said, "I'll go down tomorrow and buy another ring."

"I'm not sure that's the answer, Richard," she said at last. "I'm afraid Nan would worry just as much over the thought that her carelessness had forced you to spend money you can't afford as she now is over the loss of the ring."

Since Mr. Bobbsey could think of no better plan the discussion ended there, though not to the complete satisfaction of either of Nan's parents.

Bert observed that Nan was very thoughtful the next morning at breakfast. She barely tasted her toasted muffin and drank very little cocoa.

"Well, Miss Nan," said the waitress kindly, "you had better eat your bun. You'll need strength to tour this big city."

"Oh, I forgot I had anything on my plate," sighed the girl. "I've been thinking only of a beautiful diamond ring."

"Say," whispered her twin, "when do we shop for Sam and Dinah?"

Nan came out of her dream and brightened. "Yes," she replied, "we must start looking for their presents."

Bert turned to the young serving girl. "Could you suggest a place to buy a red vest?" he asked.

"A—a—red vest?" grinned the young lady.

"You know," continued Bert, "the bright red ones without sleeves."

"Oh yes," answered the waitress, "I've seen them in pictures—when men hunt with horses and hounds."

"That's right," said the twins excitedly. "Do you know where they are sold in this city?"

"You might try the Virginia Shop on the next block. Mr. Dixon, the proprietor, was a southern sportsman once, I believe."

The children thanked the helpful girl, and after gaining permission from their mother to go around the corner, they entered the sportswear shop.

Bert discovered it was a most unusual place. Figures of men in various costumes peeked out from behind large signs picturing animals and equipment. Rifles, fishing tackle, golf clubs, helmets and goggles were draped in every possible corner.

"Have you a red vest to sell?" asked the Bobbsey boy in a business-like manner to the nearest clerk.

"You mean a red flannel undergarment? A shirt, in other words—for warmth while working on the docks?"

"Oh no, sir," spoke up Nan, "we want a hunter's fancy vest for a dollar."

"A dollar!" Every clerk within hearing smiled. "Sorry, my lad, but our cheapest gentlemen's jockey vest is fourteen dollars and fifty cents."

"Oh," groaned Bert and his sister. "We haven't that much money to spend for Sam."

Greatly disappointed, the twins turned away in confusion. It was then that poor Bert had his most embarrassing moment. He backed away from the counter, and as he did so he bumped into a huge cardboard image dressed in complete fishing garb. The model fell to the floor, and the basket of imitation fish scattered in all directions. A pole with its line and hook in turn hit a heap of golf balls artistically piled up.

Bang! Bang! Bang!

Such a commotion and mess had never happened before. The store became dotted with the little white balls rolling noisily in all directions between the fish.

"Hey, you kid," cried the manager from the rear, "what's going on?" He pushed forward quickly, stepped on a rolling object and plunged headlong into another figure dressed as a tennis player. They both eventually sprawled full length on the floor.

Nan was laughing, for it was all very funny, but Bert and the manager looked very serious. Then a clerk thoughtfully suggested that the twins hurry on to look further for a red vest before more trouble should develop. The Bobbseys accepted the suggestion and hurried out.

"Oh, oh, oh," laughed Nan. "It was the funniest thing, just like the comic strips."

"That's what you think," growled her brother. "It was lucky we got out as easily as we did. It wouldn't have been so funny if the manager had made me pay for the damage. Gee! but I was clumsy."

"Well," said Nan in defense, "one can't have eyes in the back of one's head. Anyway, the place was too full of signs and other things piled up. I should think that mishap would take place every day in that crowded store."

"Now we are pretty sure we can't get a fancy red vest for one dollar," replied Bert.

"Never mind," sighed his sister, "let's look for the ring for Dinah."

Bert stopped a newsboy, who directed them to a "swell place for dollar jewelry." They easily found the big gaudily-painted store. It was very bright and cheerful looking inside. Bert wanted to look at everything, but Nan insisted that they just find the ring counter and then hurry back to the hotel.

The large, twinkling stones gave the Bobbsey lad an idea as the clerk laid out the trays of imitation jewels.

"Gee, Nan, maybe Miss Lee could use one of these on the stage. They do look very real," whispered the boy gleefully.

The pretty saleswoman overheard the remark

and smiled. "Plenty of these pieces are sold for just that purpose," she replied.

Bert's face beamed. Why should his sister worry any more? To him, whether they be genuine or paste, they all looked alike. "Let's buy one for the actress," he said aloud.

"Oh no!" cried Nan in dismay. "It would never, never do, Bert. I *must* replace the real lost jewel."

The clerk interrupted the children to inquire as to the size and shape ring in which they were interested. Nan decided a square cut crystal with tiny red stones on each side would please Dinah. Bert liked it, too, and so the present was quickly bought.

The circlet was placed in an attractive velvet-lined box and tied up. Soon the children were heading excitedly back to the hotel.

The doorman recognized the Bobbseys as they entered. "Your mother is looking for you, I think," he informed them.

While Bert and Nan had been shopping, Mr. Ken Speer had called up, and when Mrs. Bobbsey told him how worried she was about Nan, he promptly invited the girl to go with him on a "behind the scenes tour" of his favorite theatre. He said he hoped Bert would come, too.

Nan was delighted with the idea, for she loved

the theatre and had often longed to go backstage. Her twin was not sure he thought so well of the idea, but was coaxed into going by his sister.

"It will be so nice to accompany Mr. Speer," she said. "He's an expert, isn't he, Mother?"

"You'll be able to answer that question yourself soon," laughed Mrs. Bobbsey.

Fifteen minutes later the playwright appeared, and the older twins went off with him. The rest of that day Nan was so happy and interested that she actually forgot about the valuable diamond ring.

Mr. Speer first took the children to a studio where stage costumes alone were designed. Nan thought she had never before seen so many lovely clothes nor so many kinds of beautiful materials. Bert was a little bored until the playwright took him into a room where there were dozens of lights of various colors.

"This is where the dresses are put to a color test," he said. "Certain lights change them entirely. Wait until I show you."

Mr. Speer let Bert turn on several switches while he held a fluffy dance costume near the colored bulbs.

"Now the dress is green," he said, "and now it's purple," he added, moving it along.

"It's like magic," cried Bert. "Oh, what fun it would be to make electric lights like these."

Then the Bobbsey boy thought how good it would be if only by some magic he could make a red vest for Sam. An opportunity arrived most unexpectedly a few moments later, when he saw a discarded crimson vest among some other garments. He asked Mr. Speer if such pieces were ever sold.

"What do you want to buy," asked the playwright, "out of this odd collection?"

"I'd like that vest for our colored man Sam."

Mr. Speer laughed. "I'm sure we can fix it up so that you can take it back to Lakeport."

This was soon done, and Bert felt very pleased with the purchase.

"I'd about given up hope of getting one for a dollar," he said.

The artist who designed the beautiful stage clothes showed Nan drawings of some creations still to be made. One was so lovely that the girl caught her breath in admiration and cried:

"How I should like to wear a dress like that just once!"

"Some day," said the man with a smile, "when you become a great actress I will design you such a costume! Perhaps it will be even more beautiful than any of these. Who can tell?"

Nan thanked the man sweetly.

"The next step," said Mr. Speer after they had left the studio, "is to go where these gowns are modeled. Would you like that? And Bert, you can see behind the scenes of my big theatre."

"This is like a trip out of a story book. I can't believe it is really happening to us!" answered Bert happily.

A sense of unreality grew upon the children as the day wore on. When they reached the theatre where Mr. Speer's latest play was in rehearsal, they were greeted by a plump, pleasant woman whom the playwright introduced as Mrs. Wagner, the wardrobe mistress.

Nan and Bert could see that Mrs. Wagner and Mr. Speer were the best of friends. At the latter's request the wardrobe mistress showed Nan row upon row of beautiful stage costumes. These, she said, were her particular care.

"Mr. Speer writes marvelous plays," said the seamstress. "He is a great man. You are fortunate to be with such a fine person," she confided to the Bobbsey girl. The author, meanwhile, had taken Bert to see some queer mechanical devices which moved the various stage curtains.

"Do you know what he did for our family, Mrs. Wagner?" asked Nan. "He wrote a play just for us Bobbsey twins."

"Isn't that wonderful!" exclaimed the woman, smiling. "Will you bring it to this show house when it's ready for the public?"

"Oh no," cried Nan, blushing. "We aren't real actors. We are only doing it for our daddy's birthday."

"Well, that's highly commendable," said the understanding wardrobe mistress with a nod of her gray head.

Then Nan heard Mr. Speer call so she bade the woman good-bye and hastened to see the strange scene shifting. Bert was manipulating long rope lines.

Suddenly the girl found herself face to face with a painted fountain surrounded by fluttering doves. Quickly it was changed to an old street with a funny peanut vendor pushing a rickety cart. It was very confusing, and even more so when, without warning, a scene came down from above and hit the Bobbsey girl on the ear!

"Ouch!" she cried. "Bert! Stop! Stop!"

Mr. Speer sprang beside the fumbling boy and jerked the heavy back drop upward. Bert was very sorry of course that he had pulled the wrong line, and Nan forgave him.

"Well, I guess we've had enough of this," said the playwright. He glanced at his watch and gave an exclamation of dismay. "By Jove, I promised your family to meet them at the newspaper office at four o'clock and it's past that time now. We'll have to hustle."

When the children arrived at the office of the great newspaper to which Mr. Speer hurried them they found the rest of the Bobbsey family already there. Freddie had been over the whole plant and was thrilled by his experience.

He could talk of nothing but the presses, which he called giant rolling pins. "The funnies come right out of them, pressed flat and all colored and everything," the little fellow told Nan. "When I grow up," he added solemnly, "I'm going to be a newspaperman!"

"In the meantime," laughed Mr. Ken Speer, "how would you like to have your pictures taken? Here is the man who is head of the photographic department. He wants to snap the Bobbsey family, and put their picture in the morning paper."

CHAPTER XX

"Our pictures!" said the Bobbsey twins.

"You mean all of us?" Flossie asked, wide-eyed.

"Why not?" returned the playwright teasingly. "I don't know of anyone who would look nicer in the paper."

Mr. Bobbsey tried to protest, but the children were so eager to have their pictures taken that he finally gave his consent.

"I don't like the idea," said Mrs. Bobbsey, "and I shouldn't think of such a thing for myself, but if you say it's all right for the children, Richard, I suppose I must agree to it."

In the end the photos were taken; not once, but several times. The news photographer seemed to enjoy posing the children and took several different groups before he was satisfied with his work. Later he was heard to say to one of his friends that the little blond girl was the image of Flossie Fair.

"She is?" returned his fellow journalist earnestly. "Well, it isn't so strange at that. Everybody has his double, so it's said."

All that evening the Bobbsey twins discussed the possibility that their pictures would be in the paper the following morning. It was a fascinating thought. When they went to bed that night they were still discussing it, wondering between chuckles how they would look and what their friends back home would think of them.

"Newspaper snapshots usually look fierce," Bert warned them, "so I shouldn't expect too much."

They were up at dawn the next day, waiting for the paper to be delivered at their door. Nan was the first to snatch the news sheet when it came. She ran into her own room with it, closely followed by Bert and the two small twins. While the children gathered about her she unfolded the journal and spread it out.

"There isn't anything on the first page," cried Flossie in a disappointed tone.

"You don't expect us to be on the first sheet, do you?" laughed big-brother Bert. "Who do you think we are, anyway?"

"The Bobbsey twins," said Flossie promptly. "And I like us a lot!"

"So do I," said Freddie sturdily.

"Here we are on an inside page," cried Nan, "and it's a good picture, too, a really good picture of us all!"

There they were, in truth, both sets of Bobbsey twins, and they looked as happy as though they hadn't a care in all the world.

"What does it say, Nan?" asked Flossie.

"That the Bobbsey Twins from Lakeport are visiting in New York City," her older sister replied.

"It says too," added Bert, "that few families can boast of two sets of twins, and such good looking ones at that!"

"I'm afraid Daddy and Mother won't like that remark," said Nan. "They don't want us to get into the—what do they call it—into the public eye."

She had to explain to Flossie and Freddie that this meant calling attention to one's self so lots of people would know one. The little twins were not interested in this idea, and said they had seen enough of the paper anyway and wanted breakfast.

"I'm hungry as a wolf," said Freddie. "Gr-gr," he growled. So presently they all went down to the hotel dining room.

During the evening of that same day Flossie had a queer experience. While at the dinner table she was made to feel uncomfortable by the steady stare of a woman who sat at a nearby table. This attention embarrassed the little girl so much that she was just going to speak to her parents about it when, much to her relief, the stranger got up and left.

Undoubtedly the child would have forgotten what happened, if she had not met the woman a little later in the hotel corridor.

At the moment of this meeting Flossie was alone. She had been following her family from the dining room when she heard the clink of a piece of money on the floor. Turning about, she saw that she had dropped a penny from her little purse. As she stooped to pick up the coin some-one called her name.

"Hello, Flossie," a soft voice said.

"Hello," returned the little girl.

She straightened up to find herself confronted by the lady who had stared at her so closely in the dining room. Before Flossie had time to realize just what was happening to her, the stranger had taken her by the hand and drawn her into an elevator.

"Third floor, please," said the woman firmly, and they were lifted up with that swift motion which always made Flossie feel a little dizzy.

When the elevator reached the third floor, and

the two got out, Flossie had recovered enough
from her astonishment to protest.

"I don't want to come up here," she said.
"Mother and Daddy are downstairs. If you
please, I'd rather be with them."

"I have candy in my room," said the strange
lady. "You come with me for a little while and
I'll give you something you will like."

Still very doubtful, Flossie permitted herself to
be led along the hall. The woman stopped before
a door, inserted a key in the lock, and opened it.
Then she pushed Flossie into the room and locked
the door again very carefully, this time from the
inside.

Flossie watched her new acquaintance closely
as she flung off her coat and hat and went over to
the telephone. Before she lifted the receiver,
however, the woman turned about and faced the
little girl.

"When did you get to New York?" she demanded. Then, without waiting for Flossie to
reply, she added, "Are you going away soon?
You don't mind talking over the mike, do you?"

The little girl was so bewildered by all these
strange questions that she did not know which one
to answer first. She solved the problem, however,
by not answering any of them.

The strange young woman did not seem to

mind. Without waiting to find out whether or not Flossie would reply to her questions, she turned to the telephone and swiftly dialed a number.

"Hello," she said over the phone. "I have a scoop for you. Don't ask questions, but just listen. The famous Flossie Fair is here."

At this Flossie's eyes grew big and round. She looked about the hotel room and decided that it was quite empty except for herself and the young woman at the telephone. Where then, she wondered, was Flossie Fair?

More bewildered than ever, and beginning to feel a little frightened, Flossie Bobbsey listened to the rest of the telephone conversation. There was not very much of it. The young woman ended by saying:

"All right, I'll keep her here and write the story while your man is coming over."

The telephone receiver went back on the hook with a bang. The young woman was smiling as she turned to Flossie.

"I owe you a lot, young lady," she said. "It was mighty lucky for me that I ran into you just as I did. Have a piece of candy."

Flossie looked at the candy box thoughtfully, then put her chubby hands behind her back.

"No, thank you," she said politely but firmly.

"Oh, go ahead," the young woman urged.

"They won't hurt you. There are nuts inside them."

Still Flossie shook her head.

"If you please," she said firmly, "I'd like to go back to my mother and daddy. They'll wonder where I've gone and they're sure to worry about me."

"You may go in just a few minutes," said the stranger. "Perhaps you'll change your mind about the candy," she added. "I'll put the box here beside you so you can help yourself."

Flossie had no appetite for candy; she was growing more and more worried. She could not understand why she had to be shut up in a room with a strange woman while her mother and daddy were doubtless worrying about her downstairs in the lobby.

Meanwhile her new acquaintance had stripped the cover from a typewriter that stood on a table near the window. She was writing now at great speed, and seemed to have forgotten that Flossie was in the room.

The little girl looked at the door. The key was in the lock, but Flossie was somewhat afraid of keys; they never seemed to turn for her the way they did for other people. Oftentimes they would jam or twist, and in the end somebody else would have to come and unlock the door.

Flossie was thinking about this and getting more worried than ever, when there came a sharp knock at the door that made her jump.

Instantly the young woman left her typewriter, ran across the room, and turned the key in the lock. It worked for her, as Flossie had felt sure it would. The door opened and a young man came in carrying a big camera.

"So this is Flossie Fair," he said, and grinned at Flossie Bobbsey.

"I'm not," said Flossie with spirit. "That isn't my name at all."

"Of course that's not your real name," said the young man teasingly. "Well, I'll take some pictures of you. Stand over here, please."

"I don't want my picture taken," said the little girl, on the verge of tears. "I just *had* it taken."

In vain did Flossie protest. The young man took her picture not once but several times. In doing so he would set off some sort of fireworks with a light that made the little girl blink and a noise that made her jump. She was to learn later that this was what was called a flashlight picture.

"That's enough, Fred," said the young woman. "I guess we can let the child go."

Much to her relief, Flossie was escorted to the elevator and left to her own devices.

"I want to go downstairs, please," she said to

the amused elevator boy. "Down to the lobby where my mother and daddy are."

It seemed to Flossie that she had been a very long time in the room with the strange young woman; yet it could not have been so very long after all, for when she reached the lobby her parents were talking with some people and did not seem to be worried that Flossie had been away. So the little girl decided to say nothing of her adventure, for fear of disturbing Mother and Daddy Bobbsey, but she told her older brother a little about the queer happening.

The following morning Bert was awake early, so he dressed and went down to the hotel lobby. As he passed the newspaper stand he paused. Suddenly his eye saw something that made him gasp.

"Oh!" he exclaimed, and quickly read what was in front of him. "I—I'll take one of these," he said to the man behind the counter.

He reached into his pocket for some pennies, paid for the paper, and then hurried to his parents' room. When his father opened the door, he rushed inside and cried:

"Look at this! Just look at this!"

CHAPTER XXI

FLOSSIE'S DOUBLE

AT Bert's exclamation Mr. Bobbsey took the newspaper from his son's hand.

"What is it?" asked Mrs. Bobbsey, who was just coming through the door from Nan and Flossie's room. "That isn't the paper you usually get."

"I know it isn't," said Mr. Bobbsey angrily. "And look at this article, smeared all over the front page and featuring a picture of our Flossie. What do you think of that?"

The other children came running into the room and crowded around their mother as she sat down to read the article which had so angered her husband. There, sure enough, was a picture of their "fat fairy," and underneath it was a caption in large type:

"Famous Radio Child Arrives Ahead of Schedule. Flossie Fair's Visit in City Kept Secret."

"That's our Flossie's picture, nevertheless,"

said Daddy Bobbsey, pacing the floor angrily. "I recognize her dress. And I'd like to know how that tabloid newspaper got hold of that film."

"I guess maybe it was last night," said Flossie in a small voice. "A man took pictures of me. At least, I guess they were pictures, because he had a camera and he kept asking me to smile for him."

"Flossie Bobbsey, what are you talking about?" Mrs. Bobbsey took Flossie's arm and drew the little girl to her side. "What man do you mean, and where were these pictures taken?"

There was nothing to do then but tell of her adventure the previous evening. During the recital Daddy Bobbsey stopped pacing the floor and stared at his little daughter.

"I'm going to find that photographer," he said grimly, "and tell him a few things."

"And I'll hunt up that woman who took Flossie to her room," added his wife. "The idea!"

The telephone rang, and Mr. Bobbsey crossed the room in two strides to answer it.

"No, Flossie Fair is not in this suite," they heard him say. "She is not in this hotel. For all I know, she is not in this city!"

"This is dreadful," said the children's mother.

"There you are!" cried Mr. Bobbsey, turning wrathfully to his family. "The publicity is beginning to work already. That was a reporter from the *Star* asking for a personal interview with the famous Flossie Fair. Bah! What a joke on everybody—especially on us!"

The twins were inclined to think the whole thing rather exciting. It was fun to have a little sister who looked so much like a famous radio star. When the phone continued to ring and the manager of the hotel himself called to say that several reporters were in the lobby asking for an interview, Flossie herself began to feel very important.

It was not so much fun, though, when they were obliged to have breakfast served in their own rooms because of the publicity.

It was even less fun when they were told that they must stay in their hotel rooms all day to avoid the press of newspapermen and women who were clamoring for an interview with the famous Flossie Fair.

They got out their games, but even these seemed much less interesting than usual.

"I wish we could go outdoors," said Freddie, his nose pressed wistfully against the window glass.

"It's like being in jail," Bert said, moving restlessly about the room.

At their mother's suggestion they rehearsed the

mystery play, but it was a listless performance. It wouldn't have been much of a success, anyway, even if the children had been in the mood for it, because of the constant ringing of the telephone.

At last in desperation Mrs. Bobbsey yielded to the urging of the twins and consented to take them for a brief outing in the park. The park, fortunately, was just across the street from the hotel. By turning up Flossie's coat collar and pulling down her hat so as partly to hide her round little face, they managed to leave the hotel without attracting attention.

However, when they reached the park a nursemaid leading two small children discovered Flossie's supposed identity. Immediately, and in the most mysterious manner, the word seemed to spread through the area.

A crowd appeared from nowhere. Children and their elders pressed forward to look at the supposed Flossie Fair. Cries of "Isn't she cute?" and "What a darling. Just like a great big doll!" reached the little Bobbsey girl's ears and made her feel very shy and embarrassed.

At first Mrs. Bobbsey tried to explain to the crowd that they were making a mistake and that the little girl was not Flossie Fair. No one paid the slightest attention to her, however, and she was finally obliged to push her way by main force through the throng.

A number of reporters were waiting for them in front of the hotel. Mrs. Bobbsey saw them before they saw her, and turned back hastily, making a wide detour of the block. Then, with Flossie's hand clasped tight in hers, and the other children close at her heels, she entered the hotel by a side door.

Even then one of the reporters, more enterprising than his fellows, spied them and followed them into the elevator. Note-book in hand, and asking questions six to the second, this person pursued them down the corridor to the door of their room. He would have followed them even inside, no doubt, had not Mrs. Bobbsey gently but firmly pushed him away.

"This is awful!" said the twins' mother. She flung her purse and gloves on the bed and sat down in a chair by the window. "I guess we shall have to go back to Lakeport without Daddy after all, children. All our pleasure from now on will be spoiled by this wretched publicity."

"I don't want to go home," cried Flossie.

"Shall we have to eat dinner up here?" asked Nan.

"I presume so," said Mrs. Bobbsey. "We'll be mobbed if we try to go into the dining room."

"So here we are in jail again, just because the fat fairy looks like Flossie Fair," grumbled Bert. "I call that tough luck."

However, when Daddy Bobbsey came in a few minutes later the twins cheered up considerably. For one thing, their father said he had ordered an extra special dinner to be served to them in their room that night.

"It's really more like a feast," he told them. "You see, we're going to celebrate."

"Celebrate what?" they wanted to know.

"Well, I won my case today in court," Richard Bobbsey explained, "and I'm naturally feeling pretty good about it. Oh, and that reminds me," he added. "There's something else about Flossie Fair in the paper tonight; only it's about the real Flossie Fair this time, not our fat fairy."

Of course the twins demanded to know what Mr. Bobbsey meant. For answer their father produced a paper which contained an exciting story about Flossie Fair, the real Flossie Fair this time and not our Bobbsey twin.

"The *S. S. Northland,* New York Bound, Delayed By Heavy Storm At Sea," so read the headline. In another paragraph a little farther down was the story of Flossie Fair under the heading, "Famous Film Child Aboard *Northland* Delayed By Storm. Radio Station Fears Flossie Fair Will

Not Return In Time For First Broadcast of Season."

"Then I'll never meet her," cried Flossie. "We'll have to go home soon, and then I can't see my—my double."

CHAPTER XXII

BAD NEWS

THE news of the *S. S. Northland* and of the radio child, Flossie Fair, was received in various ways by the members of the Bobbsey Family.

Daddy Bobbsey was pleased with the whole story. He felt it would convince even the stubborn reporters of the tabloid newspaper that the real Flossie Fair was far out at sea and so could not possibly be his own fat fairy.

Mrs. Bobbsey agreed with her husband, and was happy to believe that the unwelcome publicity of the past few days was almost at an end. All the twins were disappointed, however, for they had counted upon seeing the famous child of radio who, from what they had heard, must look so much like their own fair-haired little twin.

"I did so want to see Flossie Fair," sighed Flossie Bobbsey. "And now I never shall."

The next day the Bobbseys began to pack. The twins did their part of it without wanting to, for their visit in New York had been a glorious adventure and they hated the thought of ending it.

Nan was particularly sad. Her face grew paler and paler as the morning wore on. Mrs. Bobbsey, watching her anxiously, guessed that she was worrying again about Miss Lila Lee's lost diamond ring.

"Poor Nan! This trouble about the ring has nearly spoiled her visit," thought her mother, "and mine, too," she added ruefully.

The noon mail brought the twins' mother a letter from the tourist camp where she and her family had left Waggo on their way to New York. As she opened the envelope she wondered why the man was writing to her, but the first sentence told her the reason.

"I'm sorry to say so, ma'am," the letter read, "but that there fox terrier of yours has run away. We did all we could for him. We treated him kind, I'm sure, but one day he up and followed a automobile that was passing our place. The car looked something like yours and I reckon he must have thought it was the same."

"Oh dear, our precious Waggo's gone!" wailed Flossie, when she heard the news.

Tears came to her eyes and began to run slowly down her face. "I knew we oughtn't to leave him, Mother."

"But we couldn't bring him here, dear," Mrs.

Bobbsey argued gently. "You know very well a hotel is no place for Waggo."

"What else does the man say in his letter, Mother?" asked Bert.

"Not much, I'm afraid; at least, nothing that is very helpful," said Mrs. Bobbsey, worried eyes on the scrawled sheet. "He says that Waggo may return to the tourist camp and if he does will be held for us until we call for him."

"Golly! If he never comes back he'll be lost for good," quavered Freddie. "Poor Waggo! I should have left him in Lakeport, Mother. I wish I'd never thought of putting him in the luggage carrier. If he is lost now it—it will be all my fault."

Mrs. Bobbsey tried to comfort the little lad, but Freddie was inconsolable. He even refused to eat lunch, for the first time, perhaps, in his healthy little life.

"I'm not hungry," he said, and pushed his plate away.

It was lucky for the Bobbsey family that Mr. Ken Speer dropped around that morning on his way to the theatre.

"Well, I understand from Richard that my young friends are about to desert me," he greeted them cheerily. "I don't like that at all. I think it's a shabby way to treat a pal but I thought I'd better come around and see you, anyway, before you leave."

The twins fell upon him joyfully.

"It seems to me," laughed Mrs. Bobbsey, "that you are the guardian angel of this family. Whenever any of us needs cheering up you are sure to be on hand. The children are sad this morning," she explained. "We have just heard that poor Waggo has disappeared from the tourist camp where we left him and we are afraid he is lost forever."

"Oh, nonsense," said Mr. Ken Speer reassuringly. "Dogs, especially fox terriers, almost never get lost. Waggo will turn up at the tourist camp again, never fear. And in the meantime," he added to the twins, "how would you like to go with me to a pet store where they have a lot of interesting birds and animals?"

"What kind?" demanded Freddie.

"Oh, all sorts. Rabbits and guinea pigs, goldfish, canary birds, parrots—"

"And monkeys?" asked Flossie, clapping her hands.

"Yes," said the playwright promptly. "I am almost sure I have seen a monkey there at one time or another. Well, what do you say? Shall we go?"

Of course there was only one possible answer

to that question. The twins hurried around for hats and coats and were soon ready to set out on the expedition.

The pet shop to which Mr. Ken Speer led them was a fascinating one. What a variety of birds there was! Row upon row of caged canaries lined the wall. The little songsters seemed happy and healthy filling the air with their joyous trills and piping.

"Poor little birds! It seems too bad to cage them," Nan said. "They would be much happier free."

The playwright shook his head. "I doubt that, Nan," he said. "These little creatures were born to captivity, you know, and they are happy. Probably the worst thing you could do for them would be to set them free."

"The wild birds would kill them," added Bert. "Or they'd starve because they have never learned to find food for themselves."

"Or freeze to death," Ken Speer finished. "Yes, they are much better off as they are."

There were several parrakeets in the shop and one old parrot, which hung upside-down from the top of its cage and regarded the twins with a wicked eye.

"Golly, does it talk?" Freddie asked, fascinated.

"I should think so," returned the playwright. He crooked one finger near the bars of the cage and said in a coaxing voice, "Pretty polly. Nice polly. Polly want a cracker?"

"Sixteen men on a dead man's chest," croaked the parrot. "Get out of here. Come and get it, come and get it. Ha! Ha! Ha! Oh my!"

Freddie laughed so hard he doubled up like a small jackknife. This made the others laugh just to look at him.

"Please make him say something else, Mr. Speer," begged Freddie when he had his breath back. "He must know more words."

However, the parrot would say nothing. To all their coaxing he responded only with a hoarse croak.

"I guess he must have done everything he can in that one effort," said the playwright. "Aha, what have we here?" he added, pausing before a cage which was half as big again as any of the others. "A monkey, Freddie, my lad—two monkeys. Cute little beasts, aren't they?"

"They look just like little dried-up old men," said Nan.

"Oh look, that one is making a face at us," cried Flossie, pointing to the smaller of the two marmosets. "Isn't he cute? My, but I would like that one," she added with a sigh.

"If I had a monkey I would dress him up in a little red coat and hat and teach him to do tricks and hold out his hand for pennies," said Freddie gravely. "I expect we could make a lot of money."

"Would you have a hand organ, too?" teased Mr. Speer. "Do you think your mother and daddy would like to have an organ-grinder in the family?"

"I don't suppose they would," said Freddie. "But it would be fun."

When they were leaving the store the twins stopped for a moment before a cage of cunning, roly-poly fox terrier puppies.

Guessing their thoughts Mr. Speer said kindly, "If by any chance Waggo doesn't show up at the tourist camp, I'll buy you one of these little dogs to take his place. How will that be?"

"I think you are very kind to us, Mr. Speer," said Nan gratefully.

"Thanks a lot, sir," Bert added.

Freddie said nothing, but his lips quivered as he looked at the tumbling terriers. A new puppy would be very nice, thought the little fellow, but what he really wanted was Waggo. No other dog, however cute, could be as nice as his Waggo.

Back at the hotel the twins found some very interesting news awaiting them. Mrs. Bobbsey met them in the lobby and the children could tell, the minute they saw her, that something exciting had happened.

"Mother, you haven't—found the diamond ring, have you?" Nan faltered.

"No dear, I haven't," said Mrs. Bobbsey gently. "But I have something to tell you that's a big surprise."

"Oh, what is it?" cried Freddie eagerly.

"The broadcasting company called me a short time ago," his mother replied. "They want the Bobbsey twins to put their mystery play on the air for them. Now, how's that for news!"

CHAPTER XXIII

ON THE AIR

"THE broadcasting company want the Bobbsey twins to put their mystery play on the air for them!"

Mrs. Bobbsey had really said the magic words, there could be no doubt of that. Still, the twins continued to stare at their mother for several seconds after she had made the startling announcement. They could hardly believe it was true.

"Our mystery play?" said Nan at last. "You mean they really want us to—broadcast it, Mother?"

"So they say," Mrs. Bobbsey returned, smiling at her children's astonishment. "The man at the studio who called is very much upset because Flossie Fair will not be on hand to take her part in the first broadcast of the season. He wants you twins to take her place on the program."

"Great!" said Bert. "And we'll have a lot of

fun. But why should they choose us to fill in for Flossie Fair?"

"That's perfectly clear," said Mr. Speer, who had been watching the scene with a great deal of interest. "The broadcasting company can't have Flossie Fair so they want Flossie Fair's double, who is, of course, your own fat fairy."

"You mean me," said Flossie Bobbsey with a skip of excitement. "I guess that's because I got so much 'blicity, isn't it, Mother?"

"Publicity, you mean," said Bert.

"Do you suppose Daddy will let us do it, Mother?" asked Freddie.

"I guess so," said Mrs. Bobbsey. "We'll ask him, anyway, as soon as he gets home."

Of course, Daddy Bobbsey was set upon as soon as he arrived at the hotel and was at once asked many questions. At last he became hopelessly confused and had to appeal to his wife for help.

"What are they talking about, Mary?" he asked. "I can make neither head nor tail of all this babble."

As she explained, Daddy Bobbsey listened intently, shaking his head from time to time in half-angry, half-amused protest.

"I really think it would be interesting, Richard," she pleaded. "And very instructive for the children. Do let them put on their play just this once. They will be dreadfully disappointed if you refuse."

The twins added their arguments to Mrs. Bobbsey's with the result that their father was finally won over to their side.

"I suppose it's a chance that will come only once in your lifetimes," he said with a smile. "Go ahead with your play, if you must, but be sure to put on a good performance. Remember, the honor of the Bobbsey clan is at stake!"

"We *will* put on a good performance," Bert promised.

"You bet we will," insisted Freddie, and started to recite some of his lines.

"We'll practice like anything," Flossie added.

"I hope the fellows in Lakeport will be listening in that night," said Bert. Then he added with a grin, "I guess I'd better send them a postcard so as to make sure they don't miss our show."

Word of their decision was sent to the broadcasting studio at once, and the Bobbsey twins were asked to report for first rehearsal at eleven o'clock the following morning. The children were up at daybreak, rehearsing their various parts in the play until it was time for them to go to the studio. Neither Nan nor Bert was quite satisfied with the results.

"We should have some one to act the grown-up parts," the latter decided.

"Maybe Mr. Speer and Lila Lee would take them if we were to ask them," Nan ventured. "Do you suppose they would, Mother?"

"I don't know, dear. You might suggest it, but I am afraid Ken Speer and Miss Lee are too busy with their own affairs to take part in your little play. However, you might propose it and see what they say."

Soon it was time to go to the studio. Mrs. Bobbsey ordered the car brought around, and she herself drove the children to the broadcasting building. There they were met not only by the studio manager, but by Lila Lee and Ken Speer as well.

"We want to see the fun," the playwright told them, laughing. "Miss Lee and I have a rather personal interest in the Bobbsey Twins and so we have come to watch the rehearsal, if we may."

"You may do much more than watch, if you wish," Bert cried impulsively. "Oh, please, Miss Lee and Mr. Speer, will you help? Will you take the grown-up parts for us?"

"What fun!" cried Lila Lee warmly. "How nice of you to ask us. Of course we will be delighted to appear. Won't we, Mr. Speer?"

The playwright laughed and nodded.

"Of course," he agreed. "Just tell us what to do."

"Well, you should know, Mr. Speer," said Freddie sturdily. "You wrote the play!"

Lila Lee and Ken Speer learned their parts so readily that they scarcely delayed the rehearsal at all. The play proceeded very smoothly. Everyone did well except Nan, who went through her part listlessly and often had to be prompted in her lines.

"Time out for lunch," announced the director finally. "We will all meet here at two and go through the lines again."

At luncheon Mrs. Bobbsey questioned her daughter in an attempt to find out what was wrong.

"It's the diamond ring," Nan confessed. "I think of it all the time, Mother, and sometimes it even gets in the way of the lines I have to say. I can't get it out of my mind."

"But you must try, dear," said Mrs. Bobbsey firmly. "Forget everything but the play and throw yourself into the part the way you used to do at home. I am sure Miss Lee has forgotten about the ring—for the present at least. You must attempt to do the same."

"All right," said Nan forlornly. "I'll try."

In spite of her good resolve, Nan was not able

to act any better that afternoon than during the morning. She faltered again and again in her lines and went through the performance so poorly that finally the director lost all patience with her.

"You will have to do better than that, my dear young lady," he said crisply, "or the play will be no good at all. Now, shall we try that last scene again?"

"There's no use trying. I can't do it!" cried poor Nan and burst into tears. "Please take me away, Mother. I want to go home."

"Of course, dear, we'll go right away." Mrs. Bobbsey put an arm about the weeping girl and turned to the director. "My daughter is over-tired," she explained. "She really knows her part very well, and after a good night's rest will prove it to you, I am sure. Will it be all right if I take her home now? She will be on hand in good time for rehearsal tomorrow morning."

The director was a kindly man who had two growing daughters of his own. He looked at Nan's tear-stained face and his eyes softened.

"I guess the excitement *has* been too much for her," he agreed. "Bring her back tomorrow morning and we'll go through the parts again. But remember," he added, getting back to his brisk manner, "there isn't much time left. Tomorrow night we go on the air."

In the car on the way home Bert and the little twins tried to comfort their sister.

"I wouldn't worry about the old diamond ring," said Flossie. "Miss Lee has many more of them. She had one on her finger today that was lots bigger and prettier than the one she lost at our house."

"I tell you what we'll do, Sis," proposed Bert. "Whatever money we get for this broadcast tomorrow night we will hand over to you to help buy a new ring for Miss Lee. We'll donate our share, won't we, Flossie and Freddie?"

"Sure," agreed the little twins, though Freddie asked cautiously, "I might keep out just enough to buy a new fire engine, a nice one, with lots of bright red paint."

Nan thanked her brothers and small sister for their generous offer, but she knew in her heart that all the money they would get for the broadcast would not be nearly enough to purchase a new diamond ring for Miss Lee.

That night Nan decided to go to bed early, and while she was getting ready, Flossie came into the room with a doll which she had brought with her from Lakeport. She held it up.

"Help me give Dolly a bath, Nan," she proposed.

"Oh, Flossie, I'm so tired," Nan began. Then

she stopped short as Flossie started to unwind a scarf from about the doll's neck. "Where did you get that scarf?" she demanded.

"It's your best handkerchief," Flossie said calmly. "I got it from the bottom of the pile in your box."

Nan gave a little excited scream and reached for the handkerchief.

"Give it to me, Flossie Bobbsey," she cried. "Give it to me at once!"

Alarmed by Nan's cry, Mrs. Bobbsey ran in from her room to see what had happened.

"Is anything the matter?" she demanded.

CHAPTER XXIV

FOUND!

NAN did not answer her mother at once. She was fumbling at the handkerchief with nervous fingers. Flossie, standing beside her, looked on in wide-eyed astonishment.

"Mother, there's a lump in this handkerchief," cried Nan excitedly. "Something is caught in the lace. Here it is! Oh look! Look!"

A small object rolled into the palm of Nan's hand—something that sparkled brilliantly in the light of the lamp.

"The diamond," said Nan in an awed voice. "Miss Lila Lee's diamond ring! Oh, Mother, Mother!"

With the precious ring clutched tight in her hand Nan flung herself into her mother's arms, laughing and crying hysterically.

"All the time we were looking for the ring," she gasped, "it was tied up in a handkerchief around the neck of Flossie's doll! It's silly, isn't it? But now I can give the ring to Miss Lee and everything will be all right. Mother dear, I never was so happy!"

By this time Bert, Freddie, and even Daddy Bobbsey had come in to see what all the excitement was about.

They were almost as happy as Nan when they were shown the ring. It was Mr. Bobbsey who suggested that they call Miss Lee at once and tell her of the discovery.

Fortunately, the singer happened to be at home when Nan called. The young woman was delighted at the news that the ring had been found, and promised to come over at once to the Bobbseys' hotel.

When she arrived she enveloped Nan in a warm embrace, thanked the girl gratefully for all the trouble she had gone to, and then asked to see the ring.

As Nan produced the lovely jewel her face was almost as bright as the diamond. "It *is* yours, isn't it, Miss Lee?" she asked.

Miss Lee agreed that the ring was hers.

"Although I don't deserve to get it back after being so careless as to lose it," she added. "And now, my dear," she said, reaching for her pocketbook, "I must give you a reward of some kind, although I know that nothing can really repay you—"

"Oh no, Miss Lee, please," said Nan hastily. "I couldn't take anything for finding your ring. Really I couldn't."

"Nan thinks that the pleasure of restoring your property to you brings its own reward," said Daddy Bobbsey with a smile.

"Indeed it *does*," said his daughter earnestly.

When the singer found that nothing she could say would induce Nan to change her mind and accept a reward for the return of the ring, she thanked the girl again warmly and departed, promising to meet the Bobbsey family at the studio the following day.

"I think I will be able to *act* tomorrow," said Nan, as the door closed after Miss Lee.

"And we won't have to spend all our broadcast money for a diamond ring," said Flossie.

"That's a help, Fat Fairy," laughed Daddy Bobbsey. "And now get to bed, all of you," he added. "If I am not mistaken, tomorrow will be an exciting day for all of you, including the double of Miss Flossie Fair!"

When a half hour later Mrs. Bobbsey went in to say goodnight to Nan and Flossie, she found her older daughter sound asleep. Nan's hand was beneath her cheek and there was a smile on her lips. Her mother smiled, too, and tiptoed from the room.

The next morning the twins awoke with a feeling of expectancy. Today was the great day. The hours would fly, they knew, until the momentous one which would find them before the microphone, ready to give their first broadcast over the air.

Directly after breakfast they went to the studio. There, with Mr. Speer playing the part of the father and Miss Lee that of the long-lost aunt, they rehearsed their play, "The Runaway Ring," again. Nan put so much spirit and enthusiasm into her role that the director was amazed.

"What has happened to you?" he demanded. "Yesterday you had no life, no pep. You forgot your lines and you stumbled through your part as though you were half asleep. Today everything is different. *You* are different. You play the part as it should be played."

"I'm glad you like my work," said Nan shyly. "I'll try to do even better tonight."

"Right," said the director, and turned to the others. "Now let's go through that last scene again," he proposed.

The rehearsal went so well that the director dismissed the Bobbsey twins shortly after noon, telling them to go home and get a good long rest before the evening performance.

Back at the hotel the children had a light lunch

and then went up to their rooms to rest. Flossie and Freddie made no protest when their mother tucked them into bed for naps, but they were too much excited to go to sleep.

In the late afternoon word came from the studio that it was just possible Flossie Fair might reach New York in time to broadcast after all. In this case the act of the Bobbsey twins would not be needed.

"Have them on hand, however, and ready to broadcast," the voice from the studio directed, "in case they are needed."

This news alarmed the children. Was it possible, they wondered, that they would not be allowed to broadcast, after all?

"Wouldn't it be dreadful!" cried Nan. "We've worked so hard, too!"

Dinner that night was just a confused jumble of food and talk to the young Bobbseys. They were too excited, by that time, to care what they ate, or whether they ate anything at all. They were glad when the meal was over and it was time for them to leave for the studio.

When they reached the broadcasting station the director hustled them into the studio at once. "You go on in five minutes," he told them.

"Flossie Fair hasn't come?" asked Flossie Bobbsey excitedly.

When the man said, "No, not yet," she clapped her hands in delight.

The next five minutes seemed a very long time to the Bobbsey twins. They could see Mother and Daddy in the balcony just outside the big glass partition. Daddy smiled and nodded at them, and when no one was looking Mother threw them a kiss.

The twins tried to smile back, but their faces felt queer and stiff with excitement. They wondered if they would really be able to talk into the microphone when the great moment should come.

"Flossie Fair isn't here yet, anyway," Bert whispered to Nan. "If she doesn't show up in another minute we'll be on the air."

Nan nodded and looked at the door. Mr. Ken Speer and Lila Lee came in and stood beside the children, smiling encouragement.

"How do you feel?" asked the playwright.

"I'm not scared!" said Freddie sturdily.

"I don't see Flossie Fair anywhere," said Flossie Bobbsey, her face pink with excitement. "I guess she isn't coming."

"Sh!" warned Nan, as a red light glowed in a little glass room next to their studio. "There's the announcer!"

A young man stepped to a microphone in the

balcony and explained to the unseen radio audience that the double of Flossie Fair was in the
studio and would, in company with her talented
brothers and sister, substitute for the star.

Then the red light glowed in their own studio.
The Bobbsey twins were on the air!

CHAPTER XXV

HOME AGAIN

FOR a dreadful moment after the red light glowed nothing happened. Flossie was petrified with "mike fright." She forgot that this was her cue and that she was supposed to open the scene with a burst of pitiful weeping. She forgot the people listening in, and her own parents, who were watching her so anxiously from the glass-partitioned balcony. All Flossie knew at that moment was that she was a very frightened little girl; that the studio was strange, and the microphone more terrifying than a fire-eating dragon!

Nan nudged her sister from behind, and made motions for Flossie to cry. The little girl gulped once or twice and then plunged desperately into the opening scene. She wept pitifully.

It was not so bad when Nan gave her speech about the long-lost aunt. Flossie found the going very much easier after that had been done, and by the time Mr. Ken Speer entered the scene in his role of father of the family the little girl was quite at her ease. The microphone, she had discovered, was not a fire-eating dragon after all!

The play rushed on to its happy climax—the discovery of the diamond ring, when Bert barked so fine for the dog's part. The twins performed well, not once forgetting to come in at the right cue or to speak their lines at the proper time.

Miss Lee and Ken Speer were splendid, of course, in their parts. All in all, the play was a great success, and when the final lines were spoken, there was a hearty burst of applause from those in the gallery.

A minute later, as the Bobbsey twins were about to leave the studio, a door was flung open and a little fair-haired girl rushed in. The new-comer ran up to Flossie and threw two chubby arms about the little Bobbsey girl's neck.

"You were awfully good!" said the child. "I heard your mystery play on my way up here in a taxi. The taxicab had a radio in it."

Flossie smiled at the other child.

"You must be Flossie Fair," said the little fat fairy gravely.

"And *you* are my double," returned the radio child, clapping her hands delightedly. "You look even more like me than the papers said you did. I guess I'd better 'dopt you as my twin sister."

"Oh, could you?" cried Flossie in great delight.

"That would be fun. Then I'd have a twin brother and a twin sister!"

Their elders looked on smilingly while the two little girls who seemed so much alike hugged each other again and vowed eternal friendship.

"Just the same," said Bert to Nan a few minutes later, "it's lucky for us that Flossie Fair came just when she did. Half an hour earlier her arrival would have wrecked our broadcast."

Nan nodded. "It's been a wonderful day," she added, "any way you look at it."

The next morning the Bobbsey family found still another pleasant surprise awaiting them. They were all ready to return to Lakeport. Bags were packed and safely stored in the trunk compartment of their automobile. The twins, dressed for the journey, waited in the car while Daddy Bobbsey returned the room keys and paid the hotel bill. They were feeling rather sad at the thought of leaving the city where they had had so many pleasant adventures.

Suddenly they saw Mr. Ken Speer turn the corner of the street and come toward them. The playwright returned their eager greeting with a smile and a pleasant word for each in turn. Then he held out a letter to Nan.

"From Miss Lila Lee, with a request that you deliver it to her sister in Lakeview," he explained. "And in the meantime," he added, smiling as though at a great joke which only he understood, "do you mean to say you haven't noticed anything strange about your car?"

"Strange?" echoed Nan, puzzled. "Why no. What do you mean, Mr. Speer?"

For answer the playwright reached out his hand, turned a knob on the dashboard, and instantly the automobile was flooded with music.

"Golly!" cried Freddie. "It's a radio!"

"A good one, too," smiled Mr. Ken Speer. "The very best radio Miss Lee could find."

"Did she have it put in our car?" asked Nan, astonished.

Mr. Speer nodded. "As an acknowledgment of her gratitude to you for finding her diamond ring," he explained.

"A pretty swell acknowledgment," crowed Bert. "Boy, that's a radio, and no mistake!"

"Now we can have music all the way home," said Flossie with an excited bounce. "What fun!"

The Bobbsey family did have fun, too, on the trip back to Lakeport. They tuned in on the radio whenever they could find a good program. Once they even listened to a broadcast by Flossie Fair.

"Her voice certainly does sound like yours, Flossie," said Nan.

On the way home they stopped at the tourist

camp where they had left poor Waggo. They half expected to be greeted by the little dog when their car drew up at the camp. Nothing of the sort happened, however, and the proprietor told them with regret that no word had been heard of their pet since the day he disappeared.

All of them were saddened at this news. Freddie especially took it to heart. He was silent and downcast during the remainder of the trip to Lakeport.

On the afternoon of the second day the Bobbsey twins began to sight familiar landmarks. A bridge here, a building there, told them that they were on the outskirts of Lakeport and would be home soon.

"What's the use of going home if Waggo won't be there?" said poor Freddie miserably. "He always used to come out to meet us. He'd bark, too, and wag his tail. I don't want to go home at all, if Waggo can't be there!"

As Freddie said this, Daddy Bobbsey swung the car into their own street. He started to answer his little son but stopped short as a series of barks came from the direction of the Bobbsey house.

"It's Waggo!" cried Freddie, joyfully.

The little boy tumbled from the car in time to receive a flying white bullet in his arms. The bullet was Waggo, of course, half delirious with joy at the return of his beloved family.

"He followed dem Parks people all de way home from a tourist camp," explained Dinah a few minutes later as the Bobbseys gathered in the sitting room of their house. "Leastways, de Parkses noticed he was followin' dem after a while an' so dey gib him a lift de rest of de way home."

"Nellie Parks's daddy has a car that looks a lot like ours," said Nan. "I guess it must have fooled Waggo. He thought it was *our* car."

"Dinah and Sam, did you hear our mystery play over the radio?" asked Flossie as she took off her dolly's hat and coat. "We did a real broadcast," she added. "And I look just like Flossie Fair, the little girl who talks on the radio. I'm her double!"

"Do tell!" exclaimed Sam admiringly.

"And I found Miss Lee's diamond ring!" cried Nan.

"Oh, dat's splendid," said Dinah. "You sure is de wonderfullest chilluns on de whole earth. Yes sir, you sure is!"

"I'll carry the suitcase upstairs," whispered Bert to Nan a few minutes later, "with the presents for Dinah and Sam in it, and we'll unpack it up there."

"Yes," nodded his twin. "I do hope Dinah likes the ring and Sam the red vest."

"I do, too," answered her brother. "Remember our awful experiences in that sporting goods store?"

"Do I!"

They both laughed as they reached the top of the stairs.

The little fat fairy followed close at their heels. "When is Dinah going to get her present?" she questioned softly.

"Very soon," answered Nan. "We're going to get them out now."

"Goodie, goodie," cried Flossie. "I'm awfully glad, 'cause I saw a new chocolate cake on the table, and if she likes her gifts enough maybe we can each have a big piece right away."

It was only a matter of unfastening the heavy straps and snapping the lock to get to the gifts.

Meanwhile Freddie was out in the kitchen begging for a slice of the big cake. So Dinah cut the pastry into six generous servings; one helping for each member of the Bobbsey family as a homecoming treat.

Daddy Bobbsey called the children from the second floor. Then came the opening of the package containing the crystal ring for Dinah after she had passed around her cake.

"This is sure grand an' jest mah size. Thanks to you all," and she grinned a wide smile and showed her gleaming teeth.

"Now Sam, you open your box," cried Freddie excitedly. "If you don't like it I'll take it. It would be good for a fireman."

"Hush," whispered Mrs. Bobbsey. "Let Sam enjoy his surprise from New York."

The vest was a very grand surprise, and he gave his wife Dinah a grateful look, with a bow of appreciation to all the family gathered about the table.

Then Waggo sniffed the chocolate cake and begged very prettily in front of Freddie for a crumb.

"I'll give you a big piece," said the little boy, "and I'll never, never lock you in a trunk compartment again. No sir, Waggo, I'll *never* do that again," he said very earnestly as he gave his pet a layer from his sweet dessert.

The Bobbsey children were once more ready to settle down to staying in Lakeport with their friends and pets. But after a while they were to go on a vacation which is called "The Bobbsey Twins at Windmill Cottage." What fun that was to be!